SHE SAT UP, FRANTICALLY CLAWING AT HERSELF. Everywhere she touched, slimy creatures clung to her clothes and skin.

"Rrronk!" cried Minna, wakened by Nell's screams.

"Flame, Minna, flame!" Nell cried.

Obediently, Minna exhaled a stream of flame. By the flare of light, Nell looked around. The floor and walls of the cave were seething with wretched, writhing vermin.

Nell jumped from the ledge. Oozy things squished under her feet. She slipped, going down on her knees in the living sludge.

"Aach!" she cried, shivering with revulsion as she jumped to her feet once more. Minna hovered nervously.

"This way!" Nell cried, wading ankle deep through the slithering sea.

Nell hurried on, brushing roots aside as she walked. Before long she felt a small pinch and something tugged at her arm. One of the roots had snagged her sleeve. She tugged at it, but it had burrowed into the cloth like a burr. Then there was another pinch on her other arm. Rootlike suckers had begun curling out from the cave walls, all reaching for her! Nell would be trapped like an insect in a web if she didn't do something fast. . . .

The Dragonling Series
By Jackie French Koller

The Dragonling Collector's Edition, Vol. 1

The Dragonling

A Dragon in the Family

Dragon Quest

The Dragonling Collector's Edition, Vol. 2

Dragons of Krad

Dragon Trouble

Dragons and Kings

Available from Simon & Schuster

THE KEEPERS

BOOK ONE: A Wizard Named Nell

By Jackie French Koller

ALADDIN PAPERBACKS
New York London Toronto Sydney Singapore

First Aladdin Paperbacks edition October 2003

Text copyright © 2003 by Jackie French Koller

ALADDIN PAPERBACKS
An imprint of Simon & Schuster
Children's Publishing Division
1230 Avenue of the Americas
New York, NY 10020

Designed by Debbie Sfetsios
The text of this book was set in Baskerville.

Printed in the United States of America
2 4 6 8 10 9 7 5 3 1

Library of Congress Control Number 2002115952

ISBN 0-689-85591-5

To Pat, who sparked the flame

FOREWORD

This story takes place in an ancient time known as Eldearth. In the beginning Eldearth was ruled by the benevolent Immortal, Galerinn. Witches and Wizards lived side by side with Humans then. Weefolk, though elusive, were abundant, as were Dragons and Unicorns, and all Magic was good. But Galerinn had a jealous and resentful brother, Graieconn, who began spreading lies and rumors about Galerinn, enlisting supporters to help him overthrow his brother. The result was a great war that raged on for years. At last, hoping to bring the bloodshed to an end, Galerinn challenged Graieconn to a Sorcerer's dual. The dual lasted for several days until, fearing that Eldearth would indeed fall into the hands of his wicked brother, Galerinn channeled all the light of the world into himself, transforming into a scepter so brilliant that it burned Graieconn's eyes.

No longer able to tolerate even a single ray of light, Graieconn fled with his followers into the caverns beneath Eldearth where he became the ruler of Darkearth. He still dreamed of returning one day to rule all of Eldearth, but as long as the scepter burned, the light kept him a prisoner in his own kingdom.

To safeguard the scepter, Galerinn's followers built a palace to house it and appointed the most powerful Wizard among them to channel good Magic into the scepter to keep it burning. Centuries passed and generations of Imperial Wizards took their turns as Keeper of the Scepter.

This story begins toward the end of Eldearth's first Chiliad[1], and all is not well. The last several Keepers have been weaker sorts, and the current Imperial Wizard is old and ailing. The light is fading, and Graieconn's forces have been venturing out of Darkearth more and more, wreaking havoc on Eldearth. Many would-be apprentices have undertaken the quest to become the next Keeper, but all have failed, and Galerinn's followers grow ever more worried. Graieconn, on the other hand, is rejoicing, sure that he will soon be freed from his underground prison.

But all is not lost. An ancient prophecy promises salvation. But the same prophecy also warns that if its conditions are not met by century's end, the new Chiliad will be born in darkness. . . .

---

[1] Thousand Years

Chapter One

Princess Arenelle—Nell, as she was often called—tossed her orb high into the air.

"Fetch, Minna!" she cried.

Minna, Arenelle's Demidragon, took to the sky in joyful pursuit. Just as Minna was about to snatch the ball from the air, Nell closed her eyes and whispered, "Whizza, whazza, wings!" Instantly the ball sprouted wings and zipped out from under Minna's nose.

"Zok?" squawked Minna in surprise. She pulled back and hovered, watching in bewilderment as the ball zigged and zagged above the courtyard.

Nell giggled. "Fetch, Minna! Fetch!" she repeated.

Minna looked down at her.

"Go ahead," Nell prompted. "It won't bite!"

With a swish of her long tail Minna darted off after the ball. Below on the ground Nell ran to and fro, guiding the ball's flight with the tip of her finger, keeping it just beyond Minna's reach. The little Dragon dove and twirled and zoomed, the pale sun glinting off her luminous purple scales. She was obviously enjoying this sport!

Nell laughed out loud.

"Ah!" King Einar came down the castle steps that led into the courtyard. He was smiling delightedly. "My little girl grows more clever every day," he said. He went over to Nell, and put an arm around her waist. "Mastering Animation at your age! No doubt you will be the star of the Academy of Witchcraft."

"I can only do very small things so far, Father," said Nell. "But I am practicing every day. I want to make you proud when I go off to school."

"Have no doubt of that, my little jewel," said the king.

Nell snapped her fingers and broke the spell she had cast over the orb. It turned back into an ordinary ball and started to fall. Minna swooped down and scooped it up, then fluttered to the ground and dropped it at Nell's feet.

"Good girl," said Nell, scratching Minna's nubby head.

"Thrummm," hummed Minna happily.

King Einar rubbed his arms and shivered, throwing a worried glance at the sun. "It's so chilly for this time of year," he said. "You should have a cloak on, Arenelle."

"I've been running too much to be cold," said Nell, but then she, too, glanced at the sun.

"The light grows paler every day," she said. "The Keeper must be very weak. What will happen if a new apprentice isn't found soon?"

King Einar shook his head, then changed the subject.

"We're not going to worry about that. Not today. Come along. All is in readiness for your celebration. One-one today! Where has the time gone?" Then a shadow of sorrow flickered across his face. Nell knew why. Her eleventh birthday also marked the eleventh anniversary of her mother's death. Queen Alethia had died during childbirth.

"I'm sorry, Father," said Nell.

"Sorry?" said the king. "Sorry for what?"

"That I'm here with you today, instead of mother."

King Einar's brow furrowed and he pulled Nell into his arms.

"Precious one," he said. "You must never think that. Not for a moment. I wish your mother were still with us, yes, but never instead of you. You are my jewel. You are my heart." He bent and kissed Nell on the top of her head, and she hugged him tight.

As she was growing up, Nell had heard occasional whisperings of regret around the court about the fact that she was born a girl. In Xandria, marriage was a sacred bond, never to be broken, even by death, so King Einar's hope for a male heir had died with Queen Alethia.

"Am I a disappointment, Father?" Nell had once asked.

"A *what*?" The king had gone white in the face.

"A disappointment, because I was not born a boy?"

"A boy!" King Einar had boomed. "Wherever did you get such an idea?"

"I have overheard things," said Nell. "There are

those who lament that you will never have a male heir."

"Who?" King Einar had demanded, leaping to his feet.

"I . . . I'm not sure," Nell had replied. She had not wished anyone to suffer punishment on her account.

The king would not be calmed, though. He had put the entire court on rations of bread and water for two weeks and warned that if anyone ever again expressed such an opinion, that person's mouth would be sewn shut!

Nell doubted her father would have gone to such an extreme, but no one at court seemed inclined to take the chance. Since then, everyone had made a regular practice of praising her for having had the good sense to be born a girl.

"Now come along," repeated the king. He took Nell's hand. "Your guests await."

Nell walked with her father into the castle. Minna fluttered along behind them. When they reached the door to the great hall, Lady Fidelia was waiting.

"Oh dear, now look," she fussed. "You've mussed your skirts, Arenelle, and your hair is a fright. What have you been doing?"

"Just playing in the garden with Minna."

Lady Fidelia clucked her tongue. "Well, let me straighten you up a bit," she said. She pulled her wand from her sleeve pocket and waved it a few times over Nell's head. "Scrub and comb and freshen, too," she said. "Make the princess look like new." Instantly Nell's gown was smooth and clean again and her long, black braid was undone, brushed out, and perfectly replaited.

"*Now* you look like a princess," said Lady Fidelia. "Come along."

Lady Fidelia pushed the door open and a great cheer rang out. The hall was crowded with Witches, Wizards, and Humanfolk. All the members of the court were there, plus lords and ladies from the far-flung villages of Xandria. Visiting dignitaries from many other kingdoms were in attendance as well. Xandria was the wealthiest and most powerful kingdom on Eldearth, and many rulers courted King Einar's favor.

"Happy Birthday!" they cheered. "Long live Princess Arenelle!"

Nell curtseyed and waved.

It was a festive scene with the Womenfolk and Witches in shimmering gowns and elaborate head-pieces, the Menfolk and Wizards in splendid Montue[2]-trimmed robes.

The room was decked with ribbons and flowers and glowing illusions of stars and rainbows. Fiddlers and flute players strolled about, and sweetly singing sylphs floated in the air, strumming their lutes. A great table ran the length of the room, laden with food and wine. Its centerpiece was a magnificent cake, baked in the image of a golden-crested Dragon, complete with flailing tail and flaming breath.

Despite all the merriment, however, Nell could sense

---

[2] Pure white fur of a bear-like creature

an undercurrent of worry. There were so many absent this year—those who had been killed or injured in the raids, and those who were too frightened to travel. Lately one kingdom or another had been under attack almost daily, it seemed. The forces of Darkearth had grown terribly powerful.

"Presents!" shouted King Einar. He led the way up onto the throne platform and sat down. Nell followed and took her throne, which was to the left and slightly lower than her father's. Lord Taman, the Grand Court Wizard, assumed his place on the king's right and Lady Fidelia, Grand Court Witch, took her place to Nell's left. Minna perched on the back of Nell's throne.

"Bring on the gifts!" the king bellowed.

The guests began to come forward, bearing gifts—some Human-crafted, like dolls and books and carved animals, and some Witch-crafted, including a vanishroud, a shiny new speaking star, and a portrait of Nell's mother that smiled just for her.

"And now for the best gift of all," King Einar called out. He clapped his hands, and a servant came forward with a Montue fur pillow. On it sat a small, silver box. King Einar rose from his throne and opened the box, taking out a silver chain with a deep red, heart-shaped pendant. He lifted it over Nell's head and the stone came to rest against her chest.

"It was your mother's," said King Einar softly, talking just to Nell. "She always wore it next to her heart. When she . . . when you were born, she instructed me to give it to you. For years I thought you too young and feared you might lose it. But you are a young lady now, soon to go out into the world. It is time."

Nell pressed the stone against her heart.

"Mother's?" she said.

The king nodded, and Nell's eyes widened. The stone began to grow warm.

"I can feel it," she whispered.

"What?" asked the king.

"Mother's heart," said Nell. "I can feel it beating."

King Einar nodded and smiled.

"She is with you," he said. "Turn to her whenever you are in need."

With that there came a sound of distant wailing, then a dark shadow fell over the castle.

Chapter Two

"Banshees!" shouted King Einar.

There were cries and shrieks and everyone began scurrying about, barring doors and windows.

The wailing grew louder.

"Light!" yelled the king. "Light the lamps!"

Great oil lamps were lit and dragged into place in front of each window and door. All of the fireplaces were fed until they roared with flames. Lord Taman ran to and fro, shouting orders and making sure everything was secure.

Soon the shutters began to rattle, and great gusts of cold, dank wind found their way through the cracks and crevices. All the Humanfolk of the court retreated to the center of the room while the Witches and Wizards formed two circles, Wizards in the outer ring, and Witches in the inner. They waved their wands toward the outer walls and began reciting protective incantations.

Lord Taman conjured a Ring of Light around the throne platform to protect Nell and the king.

"Rrronk," cried Minna, fluttering down and huddling in Nell's lap. Nell stroked her gently and murmured words of assurance.

"It's just the Banshees," she whispered, "trying to ruin our celebration. They'll get tired soon and pass on. They always do."

Heavy blows began to rain down on the castle's roof. Great chunks of the gilded ceiling broke free and clattered to the great hall floor. Humanfolk ducked underneath chairs and tables to avoid being hit. Nell looked up fearfully.

"What's wrong?" she cried. "Why are the chants not working?"

"The Banshees grow stronger as the Keeper of the Scepter grows weaker," said Lord Taman worriedly. "Graieconn's forces are growing stronger."

Nell shivered at the name of the lord of Darkearth. Imprisoned by an ancient injury that left him unable to tolerate even a single ray of light, he nonetheless delighted in sending his followers aboveground to wreak havoc on the kingdoms of Eldearth.

There was a sudden crash, and a window blew open.

"Who's in charge of that window?" King Einar roared.

Two Wizards ran forward, but before they could secure the window again, a ragged, dark shape swept into the room. For a moment or two the incantations kept it at bay, but then one of the Wizards in the outer ring cried out in pain and staggered backward. The Witch behind him shrieked and crumpled to the floor as the shape swept over her. Screams of terror broke out all around the room.

"Rrronk!" cried Minna.

"Remain calm!" shouted King Einar. He jumped to his feet, pulled his sword from its scabbard, then leaped from the throne platform.

"No, sire! You must stay within the Ring!" called out Lord Taman as the king charged toward the dark shape. Lord Taman rushed after the king, but King Einar had already reached the Banshee. Lord Taman quickly grabbed a torch and thrust it at the phantom. The Banshee retreated slightly, but then there was a great gust of foul-smelling wind, and the torch went out.

"Stand back!" King Einar commanded. He plunged his great, golden sword deep into the shadowy form of the Banshee. The king immediately grabbed his hand and cried out in pain. The sword clattered to the floor, twisted and charred.

With a shriek of triumph the Banshee wrapped its ragged arms around the king's neck. King Einar tore at the filmy blackness, but his fingers only went through the Banshee and clawed at his own neck.

King Einar sank slowly to the floor.

"Father!" screamed Nell. She pushed Minna to one side, then jumped up and bolted through the Ring. With an indignant cry Minna sprang into the air and followed.

"Princess, come back!" shouted Lady Fidelia.

"No!" Nell cried out. She raced across the room and began flailing at the Banshee. It was like nothing she had ever touched before—clammy and cold, yet searing hot at the same time. Her hands felt like they were on fire. Minna darted in and out of the blackness, belching flame at the Banshee, but each little burst simply fizzled into smoke.

Lord Taman and Lady Fidelia rallied the other Wizards and Witches. They circled around chanting, "Spirits of the Sacred Light! Take this darkness from our sight!"

The Banshee only squeezed the king's neck tighter. The creature seemed to be growing before their eyes. King Einar's eyes bulged and his face turned purple. Then he gasped and his body went limp.

Nell looked around desperately. "Give me that!" she cried, grabbing Lord Taman's wand.

"Princess, no!" he protested. "That wand is too powerful! The Banshee will turn it against us!"

Nell paid no heed. She thrust the wand into the very heart of the blackness.

"Spirits of the Sacred Light! Take this darkness from our sight!" she shouted.

The shape shuddered. It released King Einar and grabbed the wand.

Nell held on to the wand tightly, and the Banshee grabbed her hand. It felt like a thousand burning needles were piercing her skin. Nell's hand began to tremble. Her grip was loosening.

"No!" she screamed, struggling to hold on. Minna hovered nervously.

"The pendant!" cried Lady Fidelia. "Try the pendant!"

With her free hand Nell grabbed her mother's pendant and squeezed. It grew warm and began to pulse and Nell felt a calming strength surge through her body.

"Spirits of the Sacred Light!" she said in a commanding voice. "Take this darkness from our sight!"

The shape shuddered again and began to moan. It shrank back from the wand and seemed to shrivel.

"Take this darkness from our sight!" Nell repeated, standing tall and tightly holding the wand and the pendant. With a high thin wail the Banshee sailed back out through the open window. Lord Taman rushed to close and bolt the shutters. Nell sagged against her father, both of them gasping for breath as the wailing faded away.

CHAPTER THREE

Nell banged away on the harpsichord, practicing her lessons. Minna whirled and twirled atop the instrument, her little claws tatta-tat-tapping in time.

The birthday celebration had ended abruptly, the guests hurrying off in the fear that the Banshees would return, or that a band of Oggles or Gworfs might follow in their wake.

Behind the closed library door a "discussion" raged between King Einar, Lord Taman, and Lady Fidelia. Nell burned with curiosity. What were they arguing about? She longed to listen at the door, but she feared that if she stopped playing, the silence would draw someone out to investigate.

"If only I had gotten as far as music in my enchantment lessons," she mumbled.

Minna tapped gleefully.

"Minna!" Nell said suddenly. "Come here." She pointed to the keyboard and Minna hopped down.

Plink! Plunk! went the harpsichord keys.

"Thrummm," hummed Minna.

"That's right," said Nell. "Dance, Minna!"

The little Dragon started tripping up and down the keys, delighted with the sounds her feet were making.

"Good girl," said Nell. She waved her finger back and forth. "Keep dancing, Minna."

While Minna plink-plunked away, Nell crept to the door.

"Surely you are convinced now," Lady Fidelia was saying. "You must give Arenelle a chance, sire."

Nell scrunched up her forehead. *A chance? A chance at what?*

"And I tell you, that's nonsense!" bellowed Lord Taman. "Can you imagine a Wizard named Nell? The Keeper is a Wizard, not a Witch."

"True," said Lady Fidelia. "But there is something special about Nell. You saw the way she controlled your wand. I daresay she displayed more courage than you."

Nell smiled. Lord Taman must be seething! He was actually her cousin, son of King Einar's older sister and the previous Grand-Court Wizard who had died defending King Einar in battle. Out of loyalty, King Einar had appointed Lord Taman to succeed as Grand-Court Wizard, even though the boy had been rather young and inexperienced at the time. Lord Taman was older now, but still relatively inexperienced as a Grand-Court Wizard.

"Of course there is something special about

Arenelle," King Einar was saying. "She's my daughter, and her mother was Queen Alethia, one of the most accomplished Witches the world has ever seen. That is a powerful combination. But Nell can't be the Promised One. She's a girl, and asking a girl to be a Wizard is like asking a dove to be a fish."

Who is this "Promised One" they are talking about? Nell wondered.

"But she's our only hope," argued Lady Fidelia. "None of the other would-be apprentices have succeeded. None even passed the First Trial. Graieconn and his legions grow stronger every day. They're even attacking *you* now. We're running out of time."

"But Arenelle doesn't bear the mark," said Lord Taman. "Even if she *could* be a Wizard, she is clearly not the One."

Lady Fidelia emitted a loud sigh. "Maybe there's something in the prophecy we don't understand," she said. "I still say we must give Arenelle a chance. . . ."

"Enough!" interrupted the king. "Give me that book. I'll have no more of this nonsense. Do you truly expect me to send a helpless child out to do battle with the likes of Graieconn?"

Nell heard a heavy book snap shut.

Do battle with Graieconn? Had Nell heard correctly? Who would expect her to do battle with the lord of Darkness?

"The king is right," said Lord Taman. "If she bore the mark of the Dove, then perhaps the matter might merit

15

further discussion. But since that is not the case . . ."

"The case is closed," put in the king, "and that's the end of it."

"I still think . . . ," Lady Fidelia began.

"I said, that's the *end* of it!" boomed King Einar.

"Yes, my lord," said Lady Fidelia quietly.

Footsteps approached the door.

Quickly Nell ran over and sat down at the keyboard again. She shooed Minna back up to the top of the harpsichord and resumed playing.

Lady Fidelia bustled out of the library.

"Males!" she grumbled disgustedly.

"Is something wrong?" asked Nell.

"What could be wrong?" said Lady Fidelia. She plunked down on the divan and picked up her needle-point. She continued grumbling under her breath as she yanked her needle back and forth through the fabric.

Nell paused, her fingers on the keys.

"What were you discussing?" she asked innocently.

"Nothing," said Lady Fidelia shortly. "Nothing at all." She tied off the blue thread she was working with. "Snip," she demanded. A pair of scissors lifted off the table and came over and snipped the thread. "Now, red," she said, and a piece of red floss floated up out of her sewing box and threaded itself through her needle.

The door opened again and King Einar strode out.

"Hello, Father," said Nell. "Is everything all right?"

"Everything is *fine,*" said the king, looking pointedly at Lady Fidelia. Then he turned to Nell. "Although I couldn't help overhearing your practice. Perhaps you've been spending *too* much time on your spells."

Nell tried to hide her smile. "Yes, Father. I'm sure you're right," she said. She started playing again, deliberately making mistakes.

Lord Taman appeared in the library's doorway.

"My, my. It seems the princess needs a bit more music instruction, Lady Fidelia," he said.

Lady Fidelia frowned. "Why, certainly," she said shortly. "A very high priority in times like these."

"Father thinks I've been spending too much time on my spells," Nell told Lord Taman.

"Well," said Lady Fidelia. "I think we can all be grateful for that—*especially* your father—who might not be *alive* otherwise."

The king flushed and looked at Nell. "Indeed I *am* grateful," he said. "But I don't *ever* want you to take a risk like that again. Do you understand?"

Clank! Nell hit a particularly sour note.

King Einar winced. "And do put in a bit more time on your music lessons, please."

"Yes, Father," said Nell.

Lord Taman cleared his throat. "Commander Boris is waiting to discuss the Banshee attack, sire," he reminded the king.

"Yes, yes, I know," King Einar muttered wearily. "Lead on then."

Chapter Four

As soon as the men were out of earshot, Nell turned to Lady Fidelia once more.

"What were you and Father and Lord Taman discussing?" she repeated. "It sounded like something of importance."

"It *was* something of importance," said Lady Fidelia. "But your father thinks it should not concern you, and I must respect his wishes."

"Please tell me," Nell begged. "I won't tell Father."

Lady Fidelia rubbed her eyes tiredly.

"I'm sorry," she said. "It is not for me to say. Now on with your practice."

Nell huffed and went back to her playing, but her curiosity continued to burn. If Lady Fidelia wouldn't tell her, she decided, she would find out for herself.

"Lady Fidelia," she said after a time, "you look drawn. I think all that Banshee business this afternoon has tired you out."

Lady Fidelia nodded. "It's true I'm not as young as I used to be. There was a time when I could hold off a gaggle of Banshees before lunch and dispel a legion of Oggles that same afternoon."

Nell smiled at Lady Fidelia's outrageous exaggeration.

"Go on and take a rest then," she said. "I won't need you before evening incantations."

"Are you sure?" asked Lady Fidelia.

"Quite sure," said Nell. "I'm just going to sit here and practice until I can play this piece perfectly."

Clang! Plunk! Nell banged on the harpsichord.

Lady Fidelia raised her eyebrows.

"Yes, well, that certainly *will* keep you busy for a while," she said. "Perhaps I shall take a nap."

"Go ahead," said Nell. "I'll be fine."

"All right," said Lady Fidelia. She took a little bell out of her pocket and put it on the harpsichord. "Just send the bell for me if you need me."

"I will," said Nell.

Nell waited until she was sure Lady Fidelia was gone, then crept over to the library door and pushed it open. There were so many big books. Which one had her father, Lord Taman, and Lady Fidelia been looking at?

She read the titles on the spines:

- *A Monarch's Guide to Ruling Well*
- *The Human and Wizard War—A Historical Perspective*
- *Cedrick's Xandrish Dictionary*

- *Humanfolk, Witches, and Wizards—Celebrating Diversity*
- *The Drakian Encyclopedia of Dragons*
- *The Book of Prophecy*

"The Book of Prophecy!" whispered Nell. "Look Minna, this must be it!"

"Graw?" said Minna.

Nell pulled the book out from the shelf and sat down on the floor. On its own accord it fell open to a well-worn page near the end. Nell began to read:

> *By the end of the first Chiliad a great struggle will rise. The Imperial Wizard, Keeper of the Scepter, will grow old and weak and the powers of Darkearth will threaten the balance. If the Imperial Wizardry is to survive, it must pass into new hands—royally born, tragedy torn, and bearing the Mark of the Dove. In these hands, the Scepter of Light will glow. From these hands a powerful new Keepership will grow. If this prophecy does not come to pass, the second Chiliad will be born in darkness.*

Nell sat back against the wall, her mind spinning.

"Royally born, tragedy torn," she murmured. "That could be me!"

"Graw?" said Minna.

Nell looked up at her. "I was royally born, and Mother died during childbirth. That's certainly a tragedy."

Then she remembered Lord Taman's words: *She's a girl. The Keeper is a Wizard, not a Witch.*

That was true, but . . . Her heart began to thump. Why *couldn't* a girl be a Wizard? Where did that rule come from, anyway? Was it a given rule or a created rule?

Nell picked up the book and read the prophecy again.

"Listen, Minna," she said softly. "It doesn't say anything about girls or boys. It just says, 'royally born, tragedy torn, and bearing the Mark of the Dove.'"

Nell looked down at her right hand, at the Charm Mark which set her apart as one of the Charmed, those capable of becoming a Witch. *Or a Wizard?* Nell's heartbeat quickened. *Why not?* Just because it had never happened before?

Nell's Mark was shaped like a crescent moon—on the back of her hand just above the webbed area between her thumb and forefinger. She twisted her hand this way and that, trying to make it look like a dove. It remained a moon.

Her heart sank. "It's not me," she mumbled. "It can't be." But then Lady Fidelia's words echoed in her ears: *Maybe there's something in the prophecy we don't understand.*

Nell pondered. Maybe there *was* something they didn't understand, and maybe there *wasn't.* But there was one thing Nell knew for sure: If she did try, there was a chance of saving Eldearth. If she didn't, the world would fall to the Lord of Darkness by year's end.

She had no choice.

CHAPTER FIVE

King Einar looked down at Nell with stormy eyes.

"You had no right to eavesdrop on our conversation!" he boomed.

Minna gave a small squawk and retreated to the top of the bookshelves.

"I know," said Nell, "but I'm not sorry. I needed to know."

"You did *not* need to know," thundered the king. "It has nothing to do with you."

"How can you say that?" Nell pointed to the open book on her father's desk. "I fit most of the description. I *could* be the Promised One."

King Einar brushed Nell's words away. "Don't be silly," he said. "You don't know what you ask."

"I know precisely what I ask," said Nell. "I ask to be apprenticed to the Imperial Wizard."

King Einar shook his head. "I'm sorry," he mumbled, "but that's impossible."

Nell bristled. "Why?" she asked. "I overcame the Banshee, didn't I? And you yourself remarked just yesterday upon how advanced my Witchcraft is."

"*Witchcraft,* Nell," King Einar emphasized. "There is a big difference between Witchcraft and Wizardry. Besides, you are just a child, hardly capable of carrying out the duties of Imperial Wizard. He is the Keeper of the Scepter, the one who maintains the balance."

"Not for much longer," Nell reminded her father. "His reign is coming to an end, and the balance is faltering. Unless the prophecy is fulfilled, the darkness will win."

King Einar got up and walked to the window.

"We don't know that for certain," he said. "There are those who dispute the writings of the prophet."

"Father," said Nell, "we have seen with our own eyes how the powers of Darkearth are winning. The light grows weaker every day, and Graieconn's followers grow stronger. Soon they will rule the day as well as the night. You know in your heart that the prophecy is true."

King Einar turned back. "It makes no difference," he said firmly. "The Imperial Wizard is called upon to make hard choices, painful choices, even cruel choices sometimes. Your heart is too soft, Nell, and besides, you do not bear the mark."

"But what if Lady Fidelia is right?" Nell argued. "What if there is something in the prophecy we don't understand? If I *am* the Promised One, I must fulfill my destiny. If I don't, all will be lost."

Her father looked at her. "And what if *you* are lost?" he said quietly. "I could not bear that."

"I won't be lost," said Nell.

"Oh, no?" asked her father. "What makes you think you can succeed where others have failed? None of the other questers passed even the First Trial. Some never returned."

Nell gulped. "Never returned?" she said. "Why?"

King Einar shook his head. "Do you think Graieconn's followers sit idly by, waiting for would-be apprentices to fulfill the prophecy? Of course not. They use all their power to prevent it."

Nell sucked in a deep breath, then she straightened her back, thrusting her chin forward. "I still have to try," she said, "or we *all* will be lost. Send me to the Imperial Wizard, at least. Let me see if he will accept me as an apprentice."

"I cannot do that," said King Einar.

"Why?" asked Nell.

King Einar came forward.

"It is not as simple as you think," he said. "The Imperial Wizard dwells in the Palace of Light, which is hidden by illusions, visible only to the most gifted of the Charmed, at certain times and in certain lights."

"How do you get to it?" asked Nell.

King Einar chuckled. "Ah," he said, "*that* is the question." Then he reached down and turned *The Book of Prophecy* to the next page. IMPERIAL WIZARDRY, it read

across the top, then in smaller letters underneath, ARTI-
CLES OF APPRENTICESHIP.

"A would-be apprentice must set forth alone in
search of the palace," King Einar read. "The quester
may not partake of any food and may drink but one
parse of water at sunset of each day. If by sunset of the
third day the palace has not been reached, the quester
has failed the First Trial and may not proceed."

"Then the other questers never even reached the
Imperial Wizard?" said Nell.

"No," said the king. "All of them failed. Some
because they were . . . interfered with, others because
time ran out."

"So, I'm the last chance," said Nell.

"You are not paying attention, Nell," King Einar said
shortly. "You are not the Promised One."

"But if I were," said Nell, "where would I start my
quest?"

"That would be for you to discover," her father
snapped. "If you were the Promised One, you would
know."

Nell sighed. "You are not being very helpful," she said.

King Einar folded his arms over his chest. "Do you
really want to leave your home and venture into the
unknown alone?" he asked.

Nell was silent for a long moment. She looked out of
the window at the rolling, green hills of Xandria. She
loved her home and her father, and she had no wish to
leave. But others had been willing to heed the call, to

make the sacrifice. If they could find the courage within themselves, then she could, too. In fact the quest might be easier for Nell than it had been for the boys who went before her. Graieconn's spies would never be looking for a girl. For once her skirts would be an advantage.

"If this is my destiny," she finally said, "I must fulfill it, regardless of my feelings." She looked up into King Einar's eyes. "I know I can *do* it, Father," she said firmly. "I may not be as big or strong as some of the others who have tried, but I'm just as smart and brave."

A glint of merriment sparkled momentarily in King Einar's eyes. "I'll not argue with that," he said.

"Then I can try?" asked Nell.

King Einar smiled and put his hands on her shoulders.

"You *are* brave and good to want to help your people," he said, "and I am proud of you."

Nell smiled.

"But we will not speak of this again," King Einar commanded. "The matter is closed."

CHAPTER SIX

Nell toyed with her dinner and then announced that she was exhausted and wished to retire early. The king kissed her good night, and Lady Fidelia accompanied her back to her chambers. When they pushed the door open, they surprised a fuzzy little gremlin playing with Minna's favorite orb.

With a squawk of outrage, Minna gave chase.

Nell laughed and watched the two creatures tearing around the room for a moment, then she sobered and turned to Lady Fidelia.

"I know about the prophecy," she said quietly.

Lady Fidelia's brows arched. "How?" she asked.

"I sneaked into the study and found the book."

Lady Fidelia shook her head. "So that's why you sent me off to nap. I should have known you were up to something."

"I spoke with Father about it," Nell went on.

Lady Fidelia's eyes went wide. "What did he say?"

"He said the matter was not open for discussion."

"What matter is that?"

"The matter of me becoming apprentice to the Imperial Wizard," said Nell.

"Ah." Lady Fidelia nodded slowly. "I see."

"Why can't girls be Wizards?" Nell asked.

Lady Fidelia shrugged. "I don't know," she said. "It's just been the way of things. It was always thought that men were bigger and stronger and could better control the more powerful wands." Then she smiled. "But you've already disproved that theory, haven't you?"

Nell tossed her head impatiently. "What other reasons are there for girls not being Wizards?" she asked.

Lady Fidelia sighed. "To be honest," she said, "there are no other reasons. No good ones, anyway. As I said, it's just always been the way of things."

"Well, I think it's time things changed," said Nell. She touched her pendant. "I'm going to try."

"Try what?" asked Lady Fidelia.

"Try to fulfill my destiny."

Lady Fidelia's brow furrowed. "If it *is* your destiny," she said, "it is not an easy one."

"I know," said Nell, "but I must discover the truth."

"You mean . . . undertake the quest?"

Nell nodded.

"But how?" asked Lady Fidelia. "The minute the king discovers you missing, he'll have everyone in the kingdom scouring the countryside."

"Then he can't know I'm missing," said Nell.

Lady Fidelia laughed. "What are you going to do, conjure up another princess?"

Nell smiled wryly. "I wish I could . . ." Then suddenly her eyes went wide. "Lady Fidelia, you've just given me an idea!" she said.

Lady Fidelia smirked. "Come now," she said. "No one can conjure another person."

"Maybe not," said Nell, "but I can do the next best thing."

Lady Fidelia put her hands over her ears.

"Don't say another word," she cautioned. "I don't want to know. I can't stop you from doing what I don't know."

Nell smiled. "Thank you, Lady Fidelia," she said. Then she pretended to stretch. "I *am* tired. Please see that no one disturbs me anymore this evening."

"Certainly, Princess," said Lady Fidelia with a wink. Then she grew somber. "I wish I could go in your place," she said.

"Your courage will be with me," said Nell. "And your wisdom. You have taught me well."

"I hope so, Princess," said Lady Fidelia. "This is not child's play you undertake."

CHAPTER SEVEN

Nell pulled her new vanishroud from its wrapper.

"Oh, it's a nice one," she said appreciatively. "You can't even see the seams!"

Minna gave up chasing the gremlin and fluttered over to investigate. Nell pulled the shroud over her head, and Minna blinked, looking left and right, then swooped down and crashed right into Nell. Minna tumbled to the floor and sat looking around in confusion.

Nell giggled. "I'm here, silly," she said, lifting the hem of the shroud until just her feet showed.

"Rrronk!" cried Minna.

"Don't be frightened," said Nell. "The rest of me is here, too." She pulled the shroud off again.

Minna shook her little head in bewilderment.

"I'm going out, Minna," said Nell.

Minna darted eagerly for the door.

"I've got a plan," said Nell. "I'm going to find someone to take my place at the Academy of Witchcraft. No one knows me there. I'll find another girl with the same build and hair color and I'll teach her to be me! Then I'll be free to go on the quest and no one will even know I've gone—not Father, not the Dark Lord—no one!"

Minna switched her tail happily. Dragons, Nell knew, were very intuitive. They understood the feelings behind words and could often pick up mental pictures. Minna had undoubtedly caught Nell's excitement.

"I'm sorry," said Nell. "I can't take you. You might give me away."

Minna sank to the floor with drooping wings.

Nell looked around for the gremlin, but it was either hiding or it had decided to go play elsewhere.

"Look," Nell told Minna, taking up one of her carved Dragons. "I'll make you a new friend to keep you company. Whizza, whazza, wings!" she whispered.

Instantly the carved Dragon fluttered into the air.

"Zah?" cried Minna in surprise. With a little squawk of delight, she took off in pursuit.

"Shhh! Play quietly," Nell warned her. "We're supposed to be sleeping!"

Nell surveyed the contents of her room, looking for something she could use as a rope. The drapery cords! Nell loosened several cords and tied them together, then she opened her jewel chest and slipped a handful of jewels into her pocket. Pulling the shroud over her head again Nell locked her chamber door from the inside and slipped out through the window. She crept to the corner of her balcony and looked down. Good! No one in sight. Tying one end of her rope to the balcony, she climbed over the edge and slid to the ground.

"So far so good," she whispered as she set off across the castle lawn. She walked boldly past the parade grounds where the night guards were practicing their evening drills, then stifled a giggle as she zipped right under the gatekeeper's nose and out through the gate.

This was fun!

The village below seemed peaceful, its colorful houses stepping in neat rows down to the market square. Beyond the market the River Xandria glittered like a silver knife, dividing the upper village from the lower, a jumble of huts known simply as the Lanes.

In the distant fields Unicorns grazed, and overhead Dragonriders winged their way home from the Hill Lands, their mounts laden with Montue pelts. Nell quickened her steps. The return of the hunters signaled that the day's end wasn't far off, and she had no desire to be caught out when the Night Things came down from the hills.

It was a mild evening and the market square was bustling. So many good smells in the air! Nell was tempted to reach out and sneak a pastry from the baker's booth. But that would be misuse of Magic, a serious crime in any kingdom of Eldearth.

She kept a sharp eye out as she walked, searching for a girl who looked enough like her to fool Madame Sofia, the headmistress of the Academy of Witchcraft. The girl would have to bear a Charm Mark, too, which made the task all the harder. Most of the Charmed now lived at court or in the manors. Ever since the devastating loss Humanfolk had suffered a few centuries ago in the Human and Wizard War, wealthier Humanfolk had been intermarrying with the Charmed and raising their Charmed children as Wizards and Witches.

Nell spied a dark-haired girl about her own height and weight, and hurried over. But as she feared the girl bore no Mark. Nell wandered on, watching hands as villagers bought and sold goods. Finally she spied a Mark! But no. The hand belonged to a tall, blond-haired girl, twice Nell's age.

Up and down the narrow streets Nell walked, seeing an occasional Charm Mark, and several likely girls, but not finding both in one body. Eventually she found herself approaching the bridge to the Lanes. She had never been allowed in the Lanes, even when accompanied by her guards. She knew she should turn back, but curiosity egged her on.

Once over the bridge she found the streets crowded and noisy, smelling of refuse, rot, and worse. The houses here were small and closely packed, little more than hovels. Ragged women sat begging in the streets—some old and toothless, some young with babies or swollen bellies. Clotheslines crisscrossed overhead, and more than once Nell had to jump as a pail of slops was dumped from an upstairs window. Housewives went about their chores or leaned out of windows to chat with a neighbor. Grubby children chased one another, laughing and shrieking, while shabbily dressed men pushed carts up and down the alleyways, hawking their wares. Others gathered in little groups, talking and smoking. Hollow eyes were everywhere, faces lined and weary.

Someone bumped into Nell's invisible shoulder. A woman hurried by, then glanced back, confused. The folds of her threadbare cloak shadowed her face, but she looked remarkably like Lady Fidelia! She was about Lady Fidelia's height and weight, too, and even walked with the same determined step. But why on Eldearth would Lady Fidelia dress in rags and come to the Lanes? Nell was tempted to follow, but a sudden commotion drew her attention. She turned to see a young boy sprinting down the narrow street directly toward her. Behind the boy ran a burly man, shouting and gesturing. Nell stepped aside, but not fast enough. The boy crashed into her, and they both tumbled into the dirt. Quickly Nell gathered her shroud around her and looked to see if anyone had noticed her.

The boy sat up, rubbing his head in confusion, and Nell saw that he bore a Charm Mark!

Heavy footsteps pounded behind Nell and she turned to see the burly man bearing down on her. She tried to scuttle out of his way, but before she could, the man tripped over her and went flying.

Instantly the boy was up and away.

"Stop! Catch him!" yelled the man to no one in particular. "He belongs to me!"

Chapter Eight

Nell was curious. Why was the boy running away and who was this man who claimed to own him?

Before she could gather her thoughts, the man struggled to his feet and took off once more. Apparently he hadn't seen the boy duck down a narrow alley because the man rushed straight on toward the bridge.

Nell hurried to the corner and peered down the alley. There was no one in sight but an old man, asleep in a doorway. But the alley was long and narrow. The boy couldn't have made it to the other end so quickly. Perhaps he had ducked into a house or was he hiding? Nell tiptoed silently, keeping a sharp eye out for movement of any kind.

Before long a tousled head peeked up from behind a rain barrel. Nell stopped and examined the boy closely. He was dirty and unkempt, and his clothes were ragged, but he had a pleasing face and bright, inquisitive eyes.

The boy peeked up higher and cocked his head, listening, then he straightened and uttered a sigh of relief. Nell noted how alike they both were in height and build. And their hair color was similar, too. Suddenly she was struck by an idea. Could she possibly teach this boy to pass for a girl? His Charm Mark was different, little more than a squiggle really, and it was on the outer edge of his left hand, rather than the inner edge of his right, but that wouldn't pose a problem. Madame Sofia was a recluse, seldom venturing outside the academy's gates. She had never seen Nell, and would simply be expecting a thin girl of medium height, with long, dark hair and a Charm Mark. The hair *would* be a problem. The boy's was only shoulder length, but Nell was sure she could overcome that somehow.

"You there," she said. "I'd like a word with you."

The boy dove back under cover, then peeked out and looked left and right, a puzzled expression on his face.

Nell giggled. She had forgotten that she was still invisible. She pulled the shroud off over her head.

"What the . . . ?" blurted the boy. "Who the clop are you?"

Nell blushed. No one had ever sworn in her presence before.

"I'm Lady Arenelle," she said, "Princess of Xandria."

"Oh right," said the boy, "and I'm King Einar. At your service, madame." He bowed a low, exaggerated bow.

"I *am* she," Nell said.

"You *am* she? What the clop kind of talk is that?"

"You must stop swearing," said Nell. "It's forbidden."

"Forbidden? By who?"

"Well, I don't know exactly," said Nell. "But it's a castle rule."

"Oh, well then," quipped the boy, "I guess I'd better learn it. I spend *so* much time at the castle."

Nell smiled. She liked this boy. He had spirit. He was obviously an uneducated street urchin, though. There was little chance he could be taught all he would need to know to take her place at the academy in just two short weeks.

"Why was that man chasing you?" asked Nell.

"What man?" said the boy innocently.

"That man who claimed to own you."

"Don't know what you're talking about," said the boy.

"Yes, you do," said Nell. "I'm the one you tripped over back there. You couldn't see me because of the shroud. The man tripped over me, too."

The boy narrowed his eyes and considered what Nell had said. "Where'd you get that shroud?" he asked.

"It was a gift," said Nell.

"Well, ain't you the lucky one," said the boy with a impudent smirk.

"Aren't I," corrected Nell.

"Aren't you what?"

Nell shook her head. "Never mind. You haven't answered my question. Why did that man say he owned you?"

The boy shrugged his shoulders. "Cuz he thinks he

does," he said. "Seems my old lady owed him money. She died a few days back, and he came to collect."

"I'm sorry," said Nell.

"Sorry for what?" said the boy.

"About the death of your . . . mother?"

"She weren't my mother," said the boy. "She just raised me is all. Says she found me on her doorstep."

"Oh," said Nell. "Well, I'm sorry just the same."

"Why?" asked the boy. "You didn't kill her."

Nell rolled her eyes. "I'm just trying to be polite."

The boy frowned. "Well, don't waste yer breath. You didn't know her and you don't know me, so you can't really be sorry, can you?"

Nell frowned too. "Are you always so surly?" she asked.

The boy looked down at himself. "What do you mean?" he said. "I had a bath just a couple of weeks ago."

Nell smiled. "Never mind," she said. "What will you do now that your . . . guardian has died?"

The boy puffed out his chest. "I'm going to be a Wizard," he said, pointing to the Charm Mark on his hand. "I'm one of the Charmed, see?"

"Yes, I noticed," said Nell. "Will you be going to Wizard University?"

The boy scuffed his toe in the dirt. "'Course not," he said. "Costs a quantum of coin to go there."

"A Wizard has agreed to take you as an apprentice, then?"

The boy cleared his throat. "Not exactly," he said.

"Then how *will* you learn Wizardry?" asked Nell.

The boy looked up. "I don't know," he said. "But I *will*. You'll see. When Owen of Xandria makes up his mind . . ."

"Owen?" said Nell. "That's a strong name. Did the old woman give it to you?"

"Nah. She jest called me Boy. The Auntie gave it to me."

"The Auntie?" said Nell.

The boy nodded. "A pretty lady who came to visit the old woman now and then. She smelled good and talked nice. The old lady said she weren't really no relation, but she told me to call her Auntie."

"I see," said Nell.

"Owen was the name of a brave knight in one of the stories she used to tell me," Owen went on. "They was better than Magic, them stories of hers. I asked her if she could teach me some. Then she asked me if I'd like to be able to read 'em myself in books."

"You can read?" said Nell in surprise. Maybe this boy wasn't as hopeless as she had thought. She was getting an eerie feeling that this meeting was no coincidence.

"Yep, I can read all right," Owen answered proudly. "The Auntie taught me."

"What became of her?" Nell asked.

"She's still around, I s'pose," said Owen, "but I don't guess I'll be seeing her no more now that the old lady's gone. I'll miss them visits, but I still have my stories at least. I'll always have them."

"I love stories too," Nell said. "We have heaps of

books at the castle. Would you like to read some?"

Owen smirked. "Back to the castle again, are we?" he said. "You don't really expect me to believe you're her, do you, traipsin' around by yourself down here in the Lanes. You don't act much like a princess."

"But I am," said Nell. She pulled out a handful of jewels and held them under Owen's nose. "And if you cooperate, Wizard University may soon be within your grasp."

Owen's eyes grew wide, then narrowed again. "Aw, them ain't real," he said.

"They are," said Nell. "Come back to the castle with me and I'll prove it."

Owen hesitated. "Even if they *are* real," he said, "why would you offer 'em to the likes of me?"

"Because," said Nell, "I have a proposition for you."

"What *kind* of a proposition," Owen asked.

Chapter Nine

Owen gaped at Nell as if she'd grown a second head.

"Let me get this straight," he said. "You want *me* to dress up in skirts and pretend like I'm a girl?"

"Yes," said Nell.

He wrinkled his nose. "Are you daft?" he asked.

Nell stiffened. "Not a bit," she said. "I've thought this out very well."

"Well, you've wasted your thinkin'," said Owen, "'cause there ain't no way this boy is putting on a dress."

Nell rolled the jewels around in her hand. "There are a lot more where these came from," she said. "Enough to pay for all four years at university, and more."

The boy stared at the jewels a long moment, then shook his head. "My buddies'd bash my brains out," he said.

"Your buddies won't know," said Nell. "You'll not be anywhere near here. You'll be at the Academy of Witchcraft."

"Witchcraft?" said Owen, his eyes widening.

"Yes." Nell nodded. "I want you to take my place. You can start learning the basics of Magic there, then go on to university when I return." She jiggled the gems in her hand.

Owen eyed the stones wistfully. "You really think they'd let me into Wizard University?" he asked.

Nell nodded. "If I were to put in a good word . . ."

Owen chewed his lip. "I don't know . . . ," he said. "Why don't you want to go to the academy yourself?"

"It's not that I don't want to go," said Nell. "It's that . . . there's something else I've got to do."

"What?" asked Owen.

"I can't tell you that. Not yet, anyway. I'll tell you when I can, I promise. Now, will you do it, *please*?"

Owen still looked doubtful.

"What if they don't believe I'm you?" he said. "What if they found out I was a boy livin' there with all them girls? They'd have my hide."

"They won't find out," said Nell. "I'll teach you all you need to know. Besides, I'm to have my own chambers at the academy. You won't actually live *with* the girls."

Suddenly, in the distance, came the thump of heavy footsteps. Nell quickly tossed her shroud over her head, then she held up one corner and motioned Owen inside.

"Hurry!" she said. "It sounds like that man again."

Owen crowded under the shroud, too, just as the

burly man appeared at the entrance to the alley. He ran forward a few steps, craning his neck left and right, then he stopped and sniffed the air. He narrowed his eyes and began walking directly toward Nell and Owen.

"He can smell us," said Nell.

"How?" asked Owen.

Nell thought it best not to mention Owen's body odor. "He's likely a Wizard," she said. "Wizards develop an especially keen sense of smell."

"C'mon then," whispered Owen, grabbing Nell's hand and pulling her along. "I know these Lanes like the back of my hand. He'll have his work cut out for him, trying to track us."

The burly Wizard broke into a run.

Owen turned a sharp corner down a narrow lane, then again into another alley. Up and down streets and alleys they went, turning and returning like rats in a maze. The Wizard could see their feet, Nell knew, and hear their footsteps. He stayed close on their heels, but he was breathing hard. Hopefully he would tire before they did.

Suddenly a large Dragon reared up before them, blocking the alleyway!

"Zow!" yelled Owen. "Where the clop did *he* come from?"

The Dragon roared and flames erupted from its mouth. Nell shrank back, but something seemed wrong. Then she realized what it was—the flames gave off no heat!

"It's not real!" Nell whispered. "He conjured it. Just keep running."

Nell and Owen ran right through the flames and between the Dragon's legs.

"Zow!" cried Owen. "You're braver than you look!"

"I just know my Magic," said Nell. "Quick! Over here." She pulled Owen into a thick clump of wither-wort. "Now duck." She and Owen crouched amongst the weeds. "He won't be able to smell us in here," she whispered. "The scent of the witherwort is too strong."

"I'll say," said Owen. "I can barely breathe."

"Then hold your breath," said Nell, "and be quiet!"

They sat silently, breathing in the strong, minty scent of the witherwort as the Wizard ran through his own conjured Dragon and stood looking about wildly.

"Say," whispered Owen suddenly. "If that guy's a Wizard, maybe he wants me to be his apprentice."

A crowd had gathered, drawn by the commotion and the Dragon. They stared at the Wizard curiously.

"Out of my way!" he bellowed, roughly shoving people aside. He ran forward a few steps, then back, looking left and right and sniffing the air.

"I don't know," whispered Nell, "but there's some-thing sinister about him. I wouldn't trust him."

At last the Wizard turned in disgust.

"Get out of my way!" he shouted again, grabbing a little girl and flinging her into the gutter. "Go home, all of you, or I'll turn you into slugs!"

The child started to scream, and a ragged woman

picked her up and hurried off with her. The other villagers hastened away too.

The Wizard stalked off, and the Dragon faded away before Nell's and Owen's eyes.

"S'pose you're right," whispered Owen. "That Dragon was smashing, though! Y'think I could learn to do that?"

"Sure," said Nell. "That's just image conjuring. I believe they teach that second year at university."

Owen's eyes sparkled. "All right then," he said. "If you really are who y'say you are, you got yourself a deal."

Nell smiled. "Great!" she said. "Now, let's get going. It'll be dark soon and there's nothing *conjured* about the Night Things."

Chapter Ten

Nell could hear the Night Things howling as she and Owen approached the castle's gate. Fortunately it was still open. The night guards were filing out as Nell and Owen slipped by, the shroud gathered close around them.

"If you really are the princess, why do ya have to *sneak* into the castle?" Owen whispered.

"Because no one knows I was out," Nell whispered back. "You, and this whole plan, must be kept secret."

"How do I know you're not just a common thief usin' me to help you steal more jewels?" Owen demanded.

"Because if I stole these, I could steal more. Why would I need you?" Nell asked.

Owen looked unconvinced, but he asked nothing more.

Nell shinnied up the rope to her balcony, then ducked low behind the railing and dropped the shroud down to Owen, who was hiding in the shrubberies below. A few moments later he joined her on the balcony.

"Safe," said Nell, as they climbed through the window and barred the shutters. "Hold well, hold strong," she chanted, running her hand along the iron bar. "Keep the Night Things away till dawn."

Owen looked around. "Well, whether we got any right to be here or not," he said, "sure 'nough feels nice to be in a big stone castle at night, instead of a flimsy hut."

"The Night Things don't get in, do they?" asked Nell, wide-eyed.

"Oh, sure," said Owen with his typical swagger. "Lots of folks have been hurt, killed even, down in the Lanes. They steal babies and carry them off, too."

Nell's mouth dropped open in horror. "You've *seen* this?" she asked.

"Well . . . no," Owen admitted. "The old lady wouldn't never let me out at night. But I've heard tales aplenty and seen the scars to prove 'em."

Nell winced. "But . . . what about the night guards?" she asked.

"Never seen a night guard in the Lanes," said Owen.

Nell frowned. "Why not?"

Owen shrugged. "Too many more *important* places need guarding, I guess."

"I . . . didn't realize," Nell said quietly.

"No," said Owen, gazing around the room once again, "I don't s'pose anybody livin' in a place like this'd realize much about life in the Lanes." He reached out tentatively and touched a shimmering statuette of a monkey that was perched playfully on the edge of Nell's desk.

"Is this gold?" he asked.

"Yes," said Nell.

"Zow." Owen whistled. Then he noticed Nell's portrait on the wall.

"Hey! That's you," he said, jerking his thumb at a portrait of Nell that King Einar had commissioned just a few months ago.

"Yes," said Nell.

"So, you really *are* her," Owen said wonderingly.

"Told you," Nell quipped.

"I know, but . . . zow! A real princess!"

Nell smiled. "A princess is just a person," she said.

"Yeah," Owen replied, smirking. "Just a rich, powerful person who can have anything on Eldearth she wants."

"Not *any*thing," said Nell softly. "Not that." She pointed at her new portrait of Queen Alethia.

Owen walked over and looked up at the painting. "Who's she?" he asked.

"My mother," said Nell.

"She's beautiful," Owen murmured.

Nell walked over and looked at the portrait, too. "That's strange," she said.

"What?" asked Owen.

"She's smiling at you," said Nell. "She's only supposed to smile for me."

"Maybe she knows how much I wish I had a mum," Owen mumbled, staring fixedly into Queen Alethia's deep blue eyes.

Nell sighed. "Me, too," she said. "She died when I was born."

Owen snapped out of his reverie. He and Nell exchanged glances, then looked away again, stung by the heartache they saw clearly mirrored in each other's eyes.

"I'm s-sorry," Owen said, stumbling a bit over the word. "I s'pose I should'a known that. I'm afraid we Laners don't pay much heed to the goings on up here at the castle."

"And I . . . I am sorry for your losses as well," Nell offered.

Owen shrugged awkwardly and his usual impudent smirk returned. "Ah, you can't really lose what you never had," he said.

"Yes," said Nell sincerely. "In this case I think you can."

Owen shoved his hands into his pockets. "Yeah, well that was a long time ago," he said abruptly. "What happens next?"

Nell nodded. "Yes," she said. "We'd better get started. We've a lot to do. We leave for the academy in two weeks." She picked up her silver bell.

"Lady Fidelia, please," she said.

With a little tinkle the bell sailed off into the air and right through the doorway.

"Zow!" said Owen. "You can do Animation?"

"Some," said Nell. "Just small things so far. Which reminds me . . ."

She looked around, but saw no sign of Minna or the enchanted toy. She went over and peeked in through the folds of her bed curtains. There was Minna, curled up, fast asleep, with the still fluttering Dragon clutched tightly in her claws.

"Tired her out, did you?" Nell whispered. She freed the toy from Minna's grasp and it fluttered out through the slit in the curtains. She snapped her fingers and it tumbled to the floor with a small thump.

Owen shook his head. "You folks are going to take some getting used to," he said.

"You haven't been around much Witchcraft or Wizardry, have you?" asked Nell.

"No, Princess," said Owen. "We don't see many folks like you down in the Lanes."

There was a rap on the door.

"You sent for me, Princess?"

It was Lady Fidelia's voice. If she *had* been the mysterious woman in the Lanes, her business hadn't kept her long.

Nell looked at Owen. "You'd best hide," she whispered. "My dressing room is through that door."

Owen scooted across the room and disappeared into the dressing room, closing the door silently behind him.

"Come in," Nell called.

Lady Fidelia poked her head into the room. "Is everything . . . all right?" she asked.

"Yes," said Nell. "I just need to borrow your wand."

Lady Fidelia's eyes widened as she stepped through the door. "But you haven't had wand instruction yet, Arenelle."

"You know I can handle a wand," said Nell. "You saw what I did with Lord Taman's."

"Well, yes, but that was an emergency," whispered Lady Fidelia, "and we were all right there. All sorts of things can go wrong if a wand is misused. Why don't you just tell me what you need, and I'll conjure it for you."

Nell shook her head. "I think," she said pointedly, "that you would rather not know what I need."

"Oh!" Lady Fidelia's shoulders slumped and she rubbed her head fretfully. "This is too much for one evening!"

"What is?" asked Nell.

"Nothing, nothing," muttered Lady Fidelia.

She seemed unusually distraught. Nell longed to ask her about the woman in the Lanes, but to do so would have revealed her own secret. Nell held out her hand.

"The wand, please," she repeated.

"Oh dear," said Lady Fidelia. "If the king ever found out . . ."

"The king won't find out," said Nell.

Reluctantly Lady Fidelia pulled the wand from her sleeve pocket. "I hope you know what you're doing, Arenelle."

"Trust me," said Nell. "I'm doing only what must be

done. I'll return the wand as soon as I'm through."

"When will that be?" asked Lady Fidelia.

"I'm not sure," said Nell. "I'll let you know. Now you'd best be gone."

CHAPTER ELEVEN

Nell locked the door behind Lady Fidelia. "All right," she called in a soft voice. "You can come out now."

Minna peeked her small head through the folds of the bed curtains.

Nell giggled. "Not you, silly," she said. "I was talking to *him*." Nell pointed to Owen, who was just emerging from the dressing room.

Minna fluttered over and hovered close to Nell.

"Who's that?" asked Owen.

"This is Minna," said Nell.

"How'd you get her?" asked Owen. "Demi's are so fast, you can't catch 'em. I know. I've tried."

"I didn't catch her," said Nell. "I let her catch me."

"What?" asked Owen.

"She flew into the garden one morning," said Nell, "and when I saw her I just sat very still—still as a statue—until she came over to investigate."

"Then you grabbed her?" said Owen.

"No, I didn't *grab* her," said Nell. "I just stared at the ground, not moving, until she came right up and nuzzled me with her nose."

"Zow! *Then* you grabbed her?" said Owen.

"No," said Nell. "I just slowly reached out and stroked her. She was startled and flew off, but the next day she came back and I gave her a honey drop and . . ."

"*Then* you grabbed her," said Owen.

"No!" Nell huffed. "I never *grabbed* her at all. She came to the garden day after day, and little by little she learned to trust me. She's been with me ever since."

"Well, I'll be swaggled," said Owen. "Will she let me touch 'er, do you think?"

"If you speak softly and move slowly," said Nell.

"Hey, little Dragon," said Owen. He reached out a grubby hand, and Minna reared back. "Easy," he said. "I don't mean no harm."

"Here," said Nell, handing Owen a honey drop from a box on her desk. "Hold your hand out and let her sniff it."

Owen did as Nell suggested.

Minna sniffed the drop and zoomed away. Then she turned and hovered a moment, looking longingly at the candy.

"Go on," Nell prompted. "He won't hurt you, Minna."

Minna fluttered back and hovered just a few inches from Owen's hand. Her tongue flicked out and scooped up the candy. In that instant Owen reached out and grabbed her.

With a loud squawk Minna unleashed her claws.

"Ouch!" cried Owen, letting go.

Minna fled to the top of the canopy bed and perched there, glaring at Owen.

"What did you do that for?" Nell yelled. "Now you've frightened her."

"Just tryin' to show her who's boss," said Owen. "Critters respect that."

Nell frowned. "Creatures respect being *respected*," she said, then she reached her arms up to Minna. "Come, Minna," she said. "I'm sorry. I won't let him grab you again."

With a sidelong glance at Owen Minna flapped down into Nell's arms.

"There, there," Nell soothed, stroking the little Dragon's ruffled scales.

"You're making a sissy of her if you ask me," said Owen. "You ought to teach her to be a fighter. People pay a fortune to see demis in the pits."

"The Dragon pits?" cried Nell. "I wouldn't set foot in one of those awful places. Watching Dragons kill and maim one another is *not* my idea of sport."

Owen shrugged. "Suit yourself," he said, eyeing Minna slyly.

"And don't go getting any ideas about Minna," said Nell. "You touch her and I'll turn you into a toad."

Owen narrowed his eyes. "You're just learning Animation," said Owen. "You can't do Transformations yet."

"Not by myself," said Nell, "but I have help." She waved the wand in front of Owen.

He cowered. "No," he cried. "Don't! I won't touch her. I promise."

Nell giggled. "I wasn't about to change you into a toad," she said. "I was going to give you a bath."

"A bath?" said Owen warily. "What kind of a bath?"

"The enchanted kind," said Nell. "Don't worry. You don't have to take your clothes off."

Owen looked tremendously relieved.

"Now, let me see," murmured Nell. She waved the wand over Owen's head. "Scrub and comb and freshen, too," she said. "Make this boy all clean and new."

Instantly Owen's tattered clothes were brand new and neatly pressed. His skin shone like it was just vigorously scrubbed and his hair was silky and clean.

"Look," said Nell, pointing toward a looking glass.

Owen stared at himself in wonder. "Well, ain't I a dandy?" he said.

"Now, you'll need a place to sleep." Nell went over and lightly tapped the looking glass with the wand. She spoke another short refrain, then motioned to Owen. "Step through," she said.

"What?" asked Owen.

"Step through," she repeated, walking past Owen

and into the looking glass. Owen followed her.

"Why, it's another room," he said, "just like yours."

"Yes," said Nell, "a mirror room. Lady Fidelia used to conjure it to amuse me on rainy days."

"Zow," said Owen. "If that don't beat all."

"No more saying 'zow' and things of that sort," said Nell. "You have to learn to talk like me."

Owen frowned. "You mean all prissy and proper?"

Nell smiled. "Exactly," she said.

CHAPTER TWELVE

"I ain't comin' out there," Owen growled.

"You *aren't* coming out here," Nell corrected.

"That's what I said," snapped Owen.

Nell sighed. "Fine, then. We'll just drop the whole thing. You can forget everything you've learned these past couple of weeks and go back to the Lanes, and you can forget all about Wizard University, too."

There was a great sigh from beyond the dressing room door, then it slowly creaked open.

Nell put a hand over her mouth to keep from laughing out loud. There stood Owen in her favorite green silk frock.

"You look . . . lovely," said Nell through her hand.

"Ah, stuff it," said Owen. "I look like a girl."

"Well, that's the point, isn't it?" said Nell.

Owen scowled.

"Come here," said Nell. "Let me see you in the light."

Owen stomped out of the dressing room, tripped on his skirts, and went sprawling.

Nell giggled and helped him untangle himself from the layers of petticoats.

"Blasted skirts," Owen grumbled. "How do you put up with them?"

Nell shrugged. "Never known different. They don't get in the way much once you're used to them. Try again."

Owen stomped peevishly across the floor.

"No, no, that won't do at all," said Nell. "You must hold your shoulders erect and walk lightly, like this." Nell walked across the room to demonstrate.

"Clop," said Owen. "If my buddies ever caught a look at me walkin' like that . . ."

"No one is going to catch a look at you," said Nell. "We leave for Madame Sofia's tomorrow. And *stop* swearing!"

Owen huffed.

"Now, let me see you walk," said Nell.

Minna was watching this whole process with interest from atop a bedpost.

Owen straightened his shoulders and minced around the room. Nell covered her mouth again. "Much better," she said, then a giggle escaped. Minna chortled.

Owen stopped and glared at Nell.

"No laughing," he said. Then he looked up at Minna. "And that goes for you, too!"

Minna dove down and hid behind Nell.

"Sorry," said Nell, biting her tongue to keep from

laughing again. "All right now. Repeat after me. I am honored to make your acquaintance, Madame Sofia."

"I am honored to make your acquaintance, Madame Sofia," Owen mimicked.

"Now curtsey," said Nell.

"Why?" asked Owen. "I thought princesses didn't have to bow to nobody."

"We don't *have* to," said Nell. "It's just polite. It's what I would do."

Owen snorted. "Well, I sure wouldn't bow to nobody if I didn't have to," he said.

"To *anybody*," Nell corrected.

"Yeah, yeah. I know. You've drilled me till I'm blue in the face."

"Well, just don't slip up," said Nell. "Now, let me see how your Animation is coming."

"Can't you conjure up lunch first?" asked Owen.

"No, I'm going to bring you back some real food from my lunch. Conjured food tastes fine and it fills you up, but it has no nutrients."

"Well, just conjure me a snack to hold me over till then or I swear I'm going to eat my shoe," said Owen.

Nell pulled Lady Fidelia's wand from her sleeve pocket and put it down on her desk.

"First Animation, then I'll make you a snack," she said.

Owen huffed, but he pointed his finger at a doll.

"Whizza, whazza, walk," he said.

The doll stood up, then fell over on its face.

"Hold your finger steady until its fully up and balanced," said Nell. "Now try again."

Suddenly there was a crackle of lightning, and it started raining *in* the room!

"What the . . ." Nell whirled around. Minna had picked up Lady Fidelia's wand and was chewing on it!

"Minna, no," said Nell. "Put it—"

But before she could finish her sentence, Owen made a lunge for the wand.

"Squawk!" cried Minna. She smacked into the monkey statue, which screeched and started careening around the room.

"Screee! Screee!" cried the now Animated monkey, ripping draperies from the window frames and flinging paintings from the walls.

"Now, look what you've done!" Nell yelled at Owen.

Minna took to the air, the wand still in her mouth.

"Minna, no! Come back!" cried Nell.

Minna flew erratically, the wand throwing her balance off. *Thump!* She bumped into the bedpost. Nell's big four-poster bed began galloping around the room, crashing into walls and leaving behind a trail of bedding. Puddles of rain were forming on the stone floor. Minna looked bewildered. She flew over and perched on Nell's shelf of carved animals.

"Give me the wand, Minna," said Nell.

Minna shook her head, whacking animals with the wand left and right. Each animal came to life, growing to full size and leaping down from the shelf.

"Zow!" shouted Owen, as a tiger leaped right over his head. A whole menagerie was soon cavorting in the room. Unicorns pranced in circles. A Dragon got its head stuck in the chandelier. A pair of bears rolled and tumbled across the floor.

"Rrronk!" Minna protested.

Boom, boom, boom, came a heavy pounding on the door. *"Arenelle!"*

Nell's eyes went wide. "My father!" she said.

Owen dove though the mirror and hid behind a dresser.

Nell swallowed hard and went to the door. She threw the latch and pulled it open. A flood of water gushed out around the king's feet. One bear charged by, then the other, knocking the king first this way, then that. Close on their heels thundered the Dragon, wearing the chandelier and dragging most of Nell's bedding in its wake. A moment later the monkey swung through the open doorway. It leaped onto the king's head, then scampered off down the corridor wearing King Einar's crown.

CHAPTER THIRTEEN

"Explain," demanded King Einar as he handed the wand back to Lady Fidelia.

"It's my fault entirely, sire," she said. "I carelessly left it in Arenelle's room where the little beast found it."

"No, Lady Fidelia," said Nell. "I won't let you take the blame. I asked to borrow the wand, Father."

"And you *let* her?" King Einar glared at Lady Fidelia.

"Well, I . . ."

"She had no choice," said Nell. "I commanded her."

"Now, Princess, you did no such thing," insisted Lady Fidelia. "I must take the blame—"

"Lady Fidelia," King Einar interrupted, "I admire your loyalty to my daughter and I will speak with you about your part in this affair later, but right now I ask you to leave us. I would speak with Arenelle in private."

"Yes, my lord," said Lady Fidelia, dipping her head and glancing worriedly at Nell.

"And please make sure that *menagerie* has been properly subdued," the king added.

"Yes," Lady Fidelia repeated. "Right away, my lord."

Once Lady Fidelia was gone, King Einar clutched his hands behind his back, walked to the window, and stood staring out in stony silence.

"I'm . . . very sorry, Father," said Nell.

The king turned to her and sighed. He unclasped his hands and rubbed his brow wearily.

"Why, Arenelle? And on your last night at home? I was coming to your room to sit with you awhile, knowing how I will miss you over the next three months while you are cloistered at the academy. Now I must spend these last precious hours dealing with this unpleasantness."

Nell swallowed the lump in her throat. She hated disappointing her father, and hated worse that she was still hiding the truth from him—a far greater secret than a stolen wand. Tomorrow she would leave on her quest.

"I really, *really* am sorry, Father," she said. That, at least, was not a lie. She *was* sorry to have to deceive him. She wished there was another way, but she was convinced that there was not. She did not want to leave with him angry at her, though. "Please forgive me," she begged.

The king sighed again. "How can I do otherwise?" he said. "I have not the heart to punish you tonight."

Nell walked over and put her arms around her

father's waist. "I love you, Father," she said. "I will try harder to make you proud." This was true, too, though not, Nell knew, in the way the king might think.

"Very well, then," said King Einar, kissing Nell on the top of her head. "Let us take a short walk in the conservatory before we retire."

Owen peeked out of the mirror as soon as the king bid Nell good night and closed the door.

"What happened?" he whispered. "Did he bash you?"

"Bash me?" said Nell. "Of course not. He doesn't ever *bash* me."

"He doesn't?" asked Owen. "How does he punish you then?"

"He takes away a privilege or confines me to my room," said Nell. Then she sighed. "But to be honest, knowing I've disappointed him is the worst punishment of all."

Owen stared at her. "Zow," he said, with a rare display of emotion. "It must be smashing to have a father."

Nell's eyes filled with tears. "It is," she said.

Owen's eyes hardened again, and he wrinkled his nose. "What? Why are you crying?"

"Never mind," said Nell, drying her tears. "Did anyone see you when they were cleaning my room?"

"Naw. It only took 'em a minute. They mumbled a bunch of Magic words, and that was it. I stayed hid in the mirror."

"Good," said Nell. "Are you all set for the morning?"

"Think so," said Owen. "Why won't you tell me what you're going to be doing while I'm pretending to be you?"

"I can't," said Nell. "Not yet, anyway."

Owen shrugged. "Okay. Hope you know what you're doing."

"Me, too," said Nell quietly. She went to her dressing table and took out a knife. Then she pulled her braid over her shoulder, and, in one quick motion, cut it off.

"What the . . . ?" Owen said, gasping. "What'd you do that for?"

"When we change places tomorrow I'll have to tie it to your hair," she said, "like this." She gathered her remaining hair and tied the braid back onto it, wrapping it round and round with ribbon.

"You mean I've got to wear that flaming tail hanging down my back?" Owen complained.

"Yes," said Nell. "I'm afraid there's no help for it. Everyone knows my hair has never been cut since I was born."

Owen looked at her wide-eyed.

"Never?" he asked.

"Never," said Nell, undoing the ribbon again. She took the severed braid in her hands and looked at it sadly. "Until now."

CHAPTER FOURTEEN

The traveling party was already assembled when Nell came down the wide front steps of the castle the next morning. Owen walked beside her, covered by the vanishroud, and Minna fluttered along behind.

Lady Fidelia and the king stood waiting by the carriage. King Einar eyed the sky worriedly.

"Such a bleak day," he muttered. "I wish it were brighter."

"Have no fear, sire," said Captain Kael of the Royal Dragonguard. "The princess is in good hands."

"Take special care when crossing Kangti," the king cautioned. "Droogs have been seen in the skies around there of late, and it's thought that a flock may have taken up residence in the mountains."

"Zow!" whispered Owen into Nell's ear. "I'd love to see me some Droogs up close!"

Nell cringed. Droogs! Flying, monkeylike creatures with vicious claws and poisonous fangs?

"We will make short work of any Droogs that cross our path, sire," Captain Kael assured the king.

The king nodded, then put his arms around Nell.

"Take care, my jewel," he whispered, kissing the top of her head.

"I will, Father," said Nell, hugging him in return.

King Einar gave her a hand up into the carriage, then Nell felt the carriage jiggle as Owen climbed in behind her. Minna fluttered in and tried to sit on the seat beside Nell. Instead she ended up perched on Owen's invisible head.

"Minna!" Nell gasped, grabbing the little Dragon just as Lady Fidelia climbed in.

The king poked his head through the window.

"All set?" he asked.

"All set," said Nell, keeping a firm hold on Minna.

"All right then," said the king, his voice breaking. "May the Scepter light your path."

Nell's eyes grew moist. "And your's, Father," she whispered.

The king pulled back and motioned to the driver.

"Away!" he called.

The driver's whip cracked and the team of Dragons leaped into the air. With a lurch the carriage followed, surrounded by a legion of Men and Wizards on Dragonback—the elite Royal Dragonguard. Nell leaned out of the window and waved and waved until the castle fell away and her father was an ant-size speck on the ground. Then she sat back, hugging Minna close and fighting back tears.

Lady Fidelia fidgeted in her seat. She had seemed unusually fretful and distracted over the past two weeks.

"Is everything all right, Lady Fidelia?" Nell asked.

Lady Fidelia bit her lip. "Arenelle," she said. "That matter we spoke of on your birthday. Are you still . . ."

"It would be best," Nell interrupted with a nervous glance at the empty seat beside her, "not to speak of this."

Lady Fidelia chewed her lip, but asked nothing more.

Minna snuggled into Nell's lap and went to sleep.

"Aaachoo!" came a sudden sneeze. It was Owen, beneath the vanishshroud.

Nell quickly clapped a hand over her mouth. "Aaachoo!" she echoed.

Lady Fidelia looked up. "Oh dear, I do hope you're not catching a cold," she fretted.

"I'm fine, really," said Nell, giving Owen a dig in the side with her elbow. "It was just a little dust." She turned her attention to the scenery flying by below, the patchwork of golden meadows, rolling farms, and quaint little villages. The great manor houses looked like toys from this height, and the Unicorn herds like colonies of ants.

Then came the devastation—whole villages leveled by Graieconn and his legions of Gworfs, Oggles, Droogs, and more. . . . Nell's father's words echoed in her ears: *Do you truly expect me to send a child out to do battle with Graieconn?*

Nell shivered.

"Are you sure you're not catching cold, Arenelle?" asked Lady Fidelia.

"Yes, I'm sure," said Nell.

"Well, why don't you close your eyes and rest a bit," said Lady Fidelia. "We've several hours ahead of us yet."

"Maybe I will," Nell agreed. She put her head back and closed her eyes.

GRRAWWWWK!

A shrill screech woke Nell in the midst of a dream. She blinked and rubbed her eyes. Minna also woke with a start.

"Everyone in the carriage get down!" came a shout from outside.

Nell's head swiveled. Dark shapes were flying by. Another Dragon screamed.

"Droogs!" Nell cried.

Lady Fidelia grabbed her arm, pulling Nell and Minna to the floor, but Nell struggled free and poked her head up again.

"I want to see," she insisted.

Then she was sorry, because what she saw was several Droogs sinking their fangs into the neck of the nearest Dragon. The Dragon screamed, then went limp, spiraling toward the ground and taking its rider with it. Other guards were struggling with Droogs as well. The Men were fending them off with swords and shooting them out of the air with arrows. The Wizards were zapping them with lightning bolts.

Thump! Something hit the roof of the carriage, then a dark arm reached in through the window. It grabbed

Nell's hair and pulled her head back. She stared into a pair of glittering, black eyes, and opened her mouth to scream, but terror froze the sound in her throat.

"Rrrronk!" screeched Minna. The little Dragon launched herself full into the creature's face, all fire and fury, her claws tearing, her breath searing.

"Greeee!" croaked the creature. It freed Nell and grabbed Minna. Then Nell saw a small flash of silver, and with a long, high-pitched cry, the creature let go of Minna and dropped out of sight. Nell peered over the door to see it tumbling head over heels toward the ground.

"Everything okay in there?" Captain Kael had pulled his Dragon up close to the carriage.

"Yes." Nell's voice came out like a squeak. She cleared her throat and willed her heart to stop pounding. "Yes," she said at last. "How about out there?"

"We lost two men and a Dragon," said the captain somberly, "but it's over now. We've routed them."

Nell uttered a great sigh, then turned to Minna, who was preening her ruffled scales.

"Thank you," she said, stroking the little Dragon's head, "and thank *you*." She looked in Owen's direction, sure that the silver glint had appeared from beneath the shroud.

"Oh, I didn't do anything really," said Lady Fidelia, getting up off the floor and straightening her skirts.

Nell smiled.

CHAPTER FIFTEEN

By noontime, as the traveling party approached the academy, Nell was exhausted. The emotions from the Droog confrontation had drained her. And her stomach was growling. Knowing her quest would begin this day, she had requested breakfast in her chambers and given it all to Owen. The rules of the quest specified no food except for one parse of water each evening at sunset. She found herself longing to be fed a sumptuous lunch and shown to her new quarters. Instead, Owen would be getting to eat and rest, and she would be venturing off, perhaps into even greater danger. She hoped she was making the right choice.

The academy stood high on a hill, only its tallest turrets visible above its cloister walls. Below it, terraced down the hillside, was the hamlet where many of the professors and academy staff lived. The traveling party set down on a small landing area just outside of the village, then wound its way through the streets, up to the academy gates.

Captain Kael dismounted and pulled on a long chord.

Bong, bong, bong, clanged a bell from a tower high up in the wall.

The gates slowly swung open and two cranky-looking guards peeked out. They nodded to the captain, then swung the gates wider to reveal a graceful, old, alabaster castle. The party passed through, and Nell found herself in the loveliest gardens she had ever seen. There were flowers everywhere, blanketing the grounds, spilling from trellises, crawling up the castle walls. Gentle Unicorns meandered freely among the manicured hedges, and tiny wood nymphs flitted among the shady vines, playing games and singing. Their voices trilled like silver bells.

"Ah," said Lady Fidelia, "it's every bit as beautiful as I remembered."

The carriage came to a halt, and a footman opened the door, helping Nell and Lady Fidelia out. Minna zipped off into the gardens with a joyful cry, and Owen climbed down silently, hidden by the shroud.

"Come along," said Lady Fidelia. "I can accompany you as far as the reception room."

Nell gestured secretively to Owen to follow, then fell into step behind Lady Fidelia. Minna fluttered down and landed on her shoulder. The footmen and royal guards brought up the rear, carrying Nell's assorted trunks and bags.

Lady Fidelia led Nell into a great room, paneled in white marble with gossamer draperies billowing at the open windows. The ceilings were blue as the sky, and cherubs smiled down from the corners, strumming small harps.

"Oh, how lovely," cooed Nell.

Minna darted delightedly from one place to another, exploring every nook and cranny.

"Minna is certainly making herself at home," said Lady Fidelia. She dismissed the footmen and guards, then touched Nell's hair. "I must leave you now," she said gently. "As you know, only the novices are allowed within these walls. Your cloistering is about to begin. For three months you can have no contact with the outside world. Madam Sofia will keep us informed of your progress by speaking star."

Nell nodded silently.

"Take . . . care, now," said Lady Fidelia hesitantly.

Nell's eyes filled with tears and she reached her arms around Lady Fidelia's waist.

"Lady Fidelia," she said, "promise me that if . . . well . . . just promise me that you will look after Father."

Lady Fidelia looked alarmed. "No talk like that, now," she said brusquely. "You're going to be just fine."

"Yes," said Nell quietly. "But promise me just the same."

Lady Fidelia's brow creased with worry. "Oh, Arenelle," she said. "I hope you aren't–"

"You'd best go now," Nell interrupted. "I can't say anything more."

Lady Fidelia nodded gravely. "All right, Princess," she said. "Just . . ."

"I know," said Nell. "Be careful. I will."

"Keep the pendant with you always," Lady Fidelia added.

Nell nodded. Then, as soon as the door closed behind Lady Fidelia, she whirled around.

"Where are you?" she whispered.

"Here," said Owen, lifting off the shroud.

Nell stifled a giggle. Owen looked so silly in her rose brocade gown with pearl-encrusted slippers on his feet.

"Don't you say what you're thinking," said Owen, narrowing his eyes, "or I swear, I'll back out this minute."

"No!" said Nell. "I wasn't thinking a thing. Honest." Then her smiled faded. "That was you that saved us back there, wasn't it?" she said.

Owen shrugged. "Just did what needed doing," he said.

"Well, thank you," said Nell. "I won't forget."

Owen nodded. "It sure was exciting," he said.

"Exciting?" said Nell. "Two men and a Dragon were killed!"

"I don't mean that so much," said Owen. "I mean flying and all. I never even flew before, and"—he looked around—"look at *this* place! It's flamin' glorious!"

"Well, you've got all sorts of new experiences ahead of you," said Nell. "Just try to remember that they're not all *supposed* to be new. Don't go gushing on about things that would be perfectly ordinary to a princess. And watch your *language,* all right?"

"I'll try," said Owen.

"Try hard," said Nell. She pulled off her braid and tied it to Owen's hair, then she opened one of her trunks and took out a small, drawstring bag. In it was her new speaking star.

"This is how I will keep in touch with you, she told Owen. "Listen for my voice in your ear. You won't be able to see me, but I'll be able to see you."

Owen nodded.

Next, Nell pulled out a waterskin and a simple peasant skirt and blouse. She had no intention of calling attention to herself by traipsing around the countryside in royal garb.

"Who's going with you?" asked Owen.

"Just Minna," said Nell, "which reminds me . . . I don't know if Madame Sofia is expecting her. If she inquires, you must say that I . . . er . . . you decided to leave her at home."

"Wait a minute," said Owen. "You're going all alone, without a guard or anyone?"

"Yes. I have to."

"Why?" asked Owen.

"It's one of the rules," said Nell.

"The rules?" said Owen. "Is this some kind of game?"

Nell sighed. "I *wish.*"

"Why do I have the feeling that you are heading into danger?" asked Owen.

Nell swallowed hard. "I don't know."

"Are you taking some weapons at least?" Owen asked.

Nell's eyes widened. "I . . . never thought about weapons."

Owen shook his head. "Well, that's just great," he said. "You're heading out all alone and you don't *think* of taking a weapon."

Nell pulled the shroud part way over her head.

"I've got my shroud," she said. "I'll be fine."

Owen sighed. He reached inside his shirt and pulled out a small silver dagger in a leather sheath. It was suspended from a chain around his neck. "Here, take this," he said.

"So that's what I saw," she said. "Where on Eldearth did you get it?"

"I've had it long as I can remember," said Owen. "I think the Auntie gave it to me. Be careful," he warned as Nell reached a hand toward the dagger. "It might burn."

"What?" asked Nell. "Why would it burn?"

"It burns anyone who tries to take it from me," said Owen, "or it would have been stolen long ago." He unfastened the dagger from its chain and held it out. "Here, it should be fine now."

"I can't take your knife," said Nell.

"Yes, you can, and you will," said Owen, tucking the small, sheathed blade into her bag. "I won't need it here behind these walls, and who knows what you might run into out there."

"But . . . I could never stab anyone," Nell protested.

"If it's them or you, you'll learn pretty quick," said Owen. "Besides, it's more than just a dagger."

"What do you mean?" asked Nell.

"You'll see," said Owen. "Just take it."

Nell fingered the dagger's silver handle.

"Thank you . . . I think," she said.

"Don't mention it," said Owen. "Just come back in one piece."

"I'll try," said Nell. Then she sighed. "Well, this is it," she said. "Are you ready?"

"Yes," said Owen, "are you?"

Nell hesitated for a moment, staring into Owen's eyes. She hadn't expected to find it hard to leave *him,* of all people, but the past few weeks had been, well . . . interesting, even fun at times. She had never had a friend before, except for Minna. Was this what friendship felt like?

Suddenly there came the hollow ring of approaching footsteps from the hall beyond.

"Madame Sofia!" said Nell. "I've got to go. Come, Minna!"

Minna fluttered down, and Nell scooped her into her arms and pulled the shroud over them both.

"Take care," Owen cautioned.

"You, too," Nell called softly as she slipped out the door.

CHAPTER SIXTEEN

Nell hid behind a clump of trees and changed clothes. She lifted a large, flat stone and hid her own clothing beneath it. She tied the drawstring bag around her waist out of sight beneath her skirts. At last she took up her waterskin.

"Erf," said Minna, peeking out from under the vanishroud.

"I know it's hot and stuffy under this thing," Nell whispered as she lifted the shroud and settled it over the two of them again, "but I can't let you out yet. Someone might see us. I'll set you free as soon as it's safe."

They were still in the academy garden. The air was sweet and melodious. Nell was so tempted to stay. But she had a destiny to fulfill. The very future of Eldearth might rest on her shoulders.

She looked in all directions. The wall was unbroken, and the two guards still flanked the closed gate. How was she to get out? Then she remembered the bell!

"Minna, you must be absolutely silent. Do you understand? *Silent.*"

"Erf," squeaked Minna in a teeny, tiny voice.

"Good," said Nell. "Not another sound until I tell you it's okay." Nell crept close to the gate, then she pointed up at the bell tower.

"Bell swing, bell ring," she whispered, slowly moving her finger from side to side.

The bell trembled a bit, but didn't ring.

"It's too heavy," Nell mumbled. "Have to concentrate harder." She squinted her eyes and focused all of her attention on the bell, staring and staring until she could actually feel the weight of it pushing against her finger.

"Bell swing, bell ring," she repeated, pushing back hard against the weight.

This time the bell tipped slowly up . . . up until it stuck out sideways. Then quickly, Nell swept her hand down.

Dong, dong, dong, went the bell.

The two soldiers exchanged surprised glances.

"Who be that?" one of them asked.

The other shrugged.

The two pulled the great gates open a crack, and stuck their heads out.

This was Nell's chance! She got a running start, barreled across the lawn, her right palm extended, and shoved the smaller guard square in the rump.

"Oof!" he cried, pitching forward and tumbling through the gate.

In a flash, Nell slipped out behind him.

"Hey!" shouted the guard, getting to his feet and scowling at his partner. "What'dya do that for?"

"I didn't do nothing, ya clumsy oaf," said the other. "You tripped over yer own big feet."

"I did not! You pushed me!"

They went on arguing like two schoolboys, and Nell giggled to herself as she hurried through the streets of Academy Village and out into the countryside.

"We did it, Minna," she whispered when she was sure she was out of earshot of the village. "Everyone thinks Princess Arenelle is cloistered at the academy. You and I are free!"

"Thrummm," sang Minna, whirring her little wings.

"Not so fast," said Nell. "I can't let you go yet."

"Rrronk," moaned Minna.

Nell giggled. "Soon," she said. "I promise."

Nell looked around. Now which way? Her father had said a true Promised One would know, but one direction seemed as likely as another, and there was no one to ask.

Or was there?

Turn to her whenever you are in need.

Nell reached inside her blouse and pulled out the pendant. She clutched the heart-shaped stone in her hand. It began to glow.

"Mother?" she whispered. "Please help me find my way."

"Saidi won't take you to Mother," said a voice.

Nell whirled. Out from behind a bush stepped a young girl about one-third her size. The girl was dressed all in brown and had large pointed ears and huge brown eyes, giving her a doelike appearance. She stared curiously at Nell as if she could see right through the shroud.

"Saidi won't help you," said the girl.

"What?" asked Nell in surprise. "Are you speaking to me?"

"No," said the girl.

"Oh," said Nell, feeling foolish. She looked around for someone else, but there was no one in sight. The girl continued to stare. "Can . . . can you see me?" Nell asked.

"Can see you. Can't hear you," said the girl.

Nell scratched her head.

"If you can't hear me," she said, "how is it that you are answering my questions?"

"Can't hear questions," said the girl.

Nell was confused.

"Don't follow Saidi," said the girl. "Saidi not help you."

"I'm *not* following you," said Nell indignantly. "And you needn't be so rude. I never asked for your help."

"Go, go!" said the girl, but oddly enough, while she was saying "go" she was gesturing "come."

"You are most confusing," said Nell. "Do you want me to come or to go?"

"Go!" insisted the girl, still beckoning.

"Enough of this," said Nell. "I must be on my way."

"No, no. Don't follow Saidi!" cried the girl.

"Don't worry," said Nell. "I'm *not* following you."

With that the girl rushed straight toward Nell. She scooted under the shroud.

"Good-bye," she said with a big grin. Then she pointed delightedly at Minna. "Dragon baby," she said. "Dragon baby so ugly! Saidi hates Dragon babies."

Nell frowned. "It's not a baby. It's a full-grown demi," she said, "and you are *quite* contrary."

"No!" cried the girl, nodding vigorously.

Nell stared at her and pondered a moment. Something was nagging at her memory. Contrary . . . contrary . . .

"Why, you're a Nebbish!" she said suddenly.

"No! No!" said the girl, nodding and grinning.

"Now I understand," said Nell. "I read about Nebbishes when I was studying Weefolk. All Nebbishes are contrary. They always say the opposite of what they mean!"

"No," the girl confirmed.

"So, you *are* going to help me?" asked Nell.

"No." The girl nodded. "Stand up." She tugged on Nell's skirt and Nell bent down.

Saidi grabbed both of Nell's ears and began to twist and pull.

"Ouch," said Nell. "What are you doing?"

"Make noise," said Saidi. "Saidi will hurt you very much." Saidi tugged and tugged and Nell felt a strange stretching sensation. It wasn't really painful. Just odd.

"There," said Saidi, letting go at last. "Now princess can understand."

"Heedle, heedle, hee!" Minna chortled.

Nell reached up and touched her ears. They were huge!

"What have you done to me?" she cried.

"Don't worry," said the girl. "Saidi will change princess back soon."

"I can understand you now!" Nell suddenly blurted. "You're making sense."

"No, *princess* making sense," said Saidi. "Saidi *always* make sense."

"How . . . how do you know I'm a princess?" Nell stammered.

"Saidi know many things. Saidi good listener. Now come."

The girl ducked out from under the shroud again and beckoned for Nell to follow. With a step as light as a Unicorn, the girl loped off through a meadow. Despite her much longer stride, Nell had a hard time keeping up. Huffing and puffing she followed the little Nebbish up and down hills, through tangled thickets, across fields and through streams until at long last they came to a very thick wood.

"Princess not need shroud now," said Saidi.

Nell took the shroud off and tucked it away. Minna zipped around in happy circles, glad to be free. The fresh air did feel good after the stuffy shroud.

"What is this place?" asked Nell.

"Oldenwood," said Saidi.

Chapter Sixteen

Nell kept turning in circles as she walked, staring and staring. "It's so beautiful," she said. "Everything is so fresh and green."

"Thrumm," hummed Minna, fluttering off in search of lunch.

Now that they were walking quietly, Nell was hearing all kinds of sounds.

Snaap! Scriitch!

"What is that?" she cried.

"Bird building nest," said Saidi.

Craack!

"Oh!" said Nell. "And that?"

"Squirrel eating nut," said Saidi.

Thump, thump, thump.

Nell looked down. Hundreds of tiny ants were marching single file across her path.

"I can't believe this," she said, stepping carefully over the column.

"Believe what?" asked Saidi.

Nell giggled. "You're used to it," she said, "so I guess it isn't special to you, but I've never heard the world so clearly before!"

Below the louder noises, Nell began to hear a softer murmur. It sounded like whispering and giggling.

"Are those voices I hear?" she asked.

Saidi nodded. "Weefolk," she said.

"Why are they hiding?" asked Nell.

"Afraid of you," said Saidi. "Afraid of Tallfolk."

"Why?" asked Nell.

"Tallfolk careless," said Saidi. "Tread on Weefolk, squish their homes.

"Can I see them?" Nell asked. "I'll be careful."

Saidi nodded, then she gestured to the shadows. "Come out," she called. "Not be afraid."

There was a rush of sound, like wind blowing through a meadow. Little heads began popping up. Stones rolled away. Logs moved. Piles of leaves scattered, and Nell saw tiny houses tucked here, there, and everywhere.

"Amazing!" She bent down for a closer look. "Hello," she said to a little group of Weefolk who had gathered to stare at her.

"Hello," they clamored in return.

"What manner of folk are you?" Nell asked.

"We be Gnomes," said a miniature man with a scruffy gray beard. "What manner of folk be you?"

"I'm Xandrian," said Nell. "One of the Tallfolk."

"Well, watch your step, Xandrian," said the Gnome, shaking his finger. "Those be mighty big feet you have."

Nell laughed. "I will."

She got to her feet and followed carefully after Saidi, threading her way through tiny village after tiny village. Pixies, Imps, Gnomes . . . Weefolk of all kinds waved and called out greetings. Many followed along. Children ran and skipped to keep up, waving and pointing delightedly at Minna.

"They are so friendly," Nell said to Saidi. "I wish we had Weefolk like this in Xandria."

"Weefolk in Xandria," said Saidi. "Weefolk everywhere. Tallfolk just don't see."

Nell looked at her doubtfully.

"True," said Saidi. "Open eyes. Will see."

They came out into a sunny meadow, bright with wildflowers. Birds sang and colorful butterflies danced on the breeze. In the center of the meadow was a magnificent, old tree, the largest one Nell could ever remember seeing. The Weefolk ran ahead and settled themselves on the ground beneath the shade of its branches.

"Mother," said Saidi.

Nell looked around. "Where is your mother?" she asked.

"Not Saidi's mother," said the Nebbish, pulling Nell after her into the shade of the tree. "Old Mother."

Nell looked about her at the upturned faces of the Weefolk. There were many old women.

"Which one is Old Mother?" she asked.

"I am," said a gentle voice.

Nell's head swiveled. "Where?"

"Here, child. You are not very perceptive, are you?"

Nell blinked. The voice seemed to be coming from the tree! "Saidi," she whispered, wide-eyed. "Could . . . could the *tree* be talking?"

"Yes," said Saidi. "Trees have much to say. Especially Old Mother."

"Why do you call her Old Mother?" asked Nell.

"Because I'm the oldest tree in the forest," said the tree, "and I would be grateful if you would address your questions directly to me."

"Um, yes, ma'am," said Nell, dropping a curtsey. "I beg your pardon, ma'am."

"That's better," said the tree. "Now, tell me child. Why have you come?"

"I undertake the quest," said Nell, "to find the Palace of Light."

"Hmm," said Old Mother. "Another would-be apprentice?"

"Yes," said Nell. "I hope to become Imperial Wizard and restore the balance."

"The balance for whom?" asked Old Mother. "Tallfolk or all folk?"

"Isn't it the same?" asked Nell.

"It should be," said Old Mother, "but it isn't. Hasn't been for centuries."

"I'm not sure what you mean," said Nell.

"I mean that the Imperial Wizardry is not what Galerinn would have wished. Galerinn was all goodness. He respected Eldearth and all folk were equal in his eyes—small, tall, weak, strong, rich, poor . . ."

Nell looked around her at the circle of Weefolk.

"Over the centuries," Old Mother went on, "the Imperial Wizardry has become so much about the tall, the strong, and the rich that the small, the weak, and the poor have become virtually invisible."

Nell chewed her lip thoughtfully, remembering Saidi's words: *Weefolk everywhere. Tallfolk just don't see.* Had Nell been blind to Weefolk all her life, just as she had been blind to the plight of the folk in the Lanes?

"I'm afraid that I have grown up rather sheltered," she said to Old Mother. "I am discovering that I have been unaware of many things."

"That is understandable for a child," said Old Mother, "but not for an Imperial Wizard."

"Maybe . . . ," said Nell. "Maybe that's what this quest is all about. Maybe I am meant to change things."

Minna, who had been playing with some children in the meadow, returned to Nell's shoulder. Absentmindedly, Nell reached up and stroked her.

Old Mother swayed back and forth as if nodding her great green head. "You *are* different from the other questers," she remarked thoughtfully.

Nell looked up. "You mean because I'm a girl?"

"No. I mean because you are humble and you listen,"

said Old Mother. "You are not full of your own importance."

Nell sensed a glimmer of hope. "Does that mean you will help me?" she asked.

Old Mother considered a long moment, then swayed again.

"Yes," she said. "I will set you on the right path. That is all I can do, but it is more than I have done for a quester in many years."

"Thank you," said Nell. "I will try hard to be worthy of your help."

"The pass lies to the south, through rugged mountains," said Old Mother. "But you cannot traverse it in three days' time. Have you no wings?"

"No," said Nell. "I have undertaken this quest in secret. There was no way to take a Dragon without calling attention to my leaving."

"Then you will have to go through the mountain," said Old Mother.

"*Through* the mountain?" asked Nell.

"Yes." Old Mother pointed to a waterfall in the distance. "There is a secret passage behind those falls, but be wary, child, the way is not easy. It could even prove the death of you."

Nell swallowed hard.

"Getting late," Saidi interrupted, looking at the sky. "Princess must hurry."

Nell looked at the sky, too. Darkness was coming on.

"Yes." She nodded. "We had best be going."

"Princess must go alone from here," said Saidi.

"You're not coming?" Nell asked, in dismay.

"Princess must go alone," Saidi repeated.

Nell sighed and nodded in resignation.

"Bend down," said Saidi.

Nell went down on one knee, and Saidi put her hands on Nell's ears and squeezed. How quiet everything suddenly became!

"Hello," said Saidi. "Be careless." Then she gave Nell a quick hug.

"Farewell," said Nell. "Until we meet again." Then she stood and looked at the tree once more.

"What lies beyond the passage?" she asked.

If Old Mother answered, Nell could no longer hear her.

Chapter Seventeen

Nell held Minna tightly and plunged through the falls. Icy water pummeled them, and Minna squawked resentfully.

"I'm sorry," Nell sputtered. "I don't like it any better than you do."

At last they emerged in a great, damp cave, lit only by the pale glow of light shimmering through the waterfall. Minna flapped over to a small ledge, perched, and shook herself from head to toe. Nell wished she could dry herself as easily.

"Hello," she called out tentatively, but the cave's only inhabitants appeared to be centipedes and salamanders. The cave funneled down to a small opening on the far side. Nell walked over and peered in, shivering in disgust as creepy, crawly things scurried out of her way. She couldn't see beyond the first few cubits of the passageway.

"I guess we'll have to sleep here," she said to Minna. "I don't have the courage or the strength to attempt that passageway tonight."

Minna yawned.

Nell scouted about for firewood, but there was nothing. At last she gave up and just looked for a place to sleep. Minna's small ledge was the only likely looking spot. It was just a narrow shelf of cold hard stone, but at least it was up off the floor.

Dark things scurried into cracks and crevices as Nell hoisted herself up onto the ledge. She shivered again, her clothing still wet from the plunge through the falls. It would not be a comfortable night.

Minna yawned a few more times, then curled into a ball and closed her eyes.

Nell opened her waterskin and took a deep drink. The refreshment cleared her head and restored her energy a bit. But she was so hungry. She'd never gone a whole day without eating before. She hoped to find the Palace of Light soon. She didn't know how she would get through two more days without food. She pulled out her speaking star.

"Show me Owen," she said. "Academy of Witchcraft."

A soft light began to glow at the center of the star. It brightened and spread until Nell could see Owen, sitting alone at a desk, poring over a book.

"Owen," she called softly.

Owen's head jerked up.

"Owen, it's me—Nell."

"Where?" asked Owen.

"I'm speaking to you through the speaking star. I told you that you wouldn't be able to see me, remember?"

"Oh yeah."

"Is anyone nearby?" asked Nell.

"No, it's study time—now until lights out."

"You've already had dinner?" said Nell.

"I'll say," said Owen. "You should see what they feed you around here. There was—"

"Please," Nell interrupted, "don't tell me."

"Why not?" asked Owen.

"Because I've had no dinner myself and it would be too hard to listen."

"No dinner?" said Owen. "Why?"

"Never mind," said Nell. "How are things going?"

"All right," said Owen. "The old headmistress is a real witch, though."

"What did you expect?" said Nell.

"No, I mean a *witchy* Witch," said Owen. "The mean kind. If she smiled I think her face would crack."

Nell laughed. "Well, just try to stay on her good side. We don't want any problems."

"You mean she *has* a good side?" asked Owen.

Nell smiled. "Do you think anyone suspects anything?"

"Nope." Owen beamed. "I got the act down perfect. They think I'm a right proper princess. Curtsied and everything."

Nell chuckled.

"What's that you're studying?" she asked.

Owen rolled his eyes.

"Love potions," he said. "What a bunch of clop."

"*Don't* swear," said Nell. "One of these times you'll forget and slip when someone else is around to hear."

"All right, then. It's a bunch of nonsense," said Owen.

"Maybe to you," said Nell. "But to someone like me, love potions are important."

Owen grimaced. "Why?" he asked. "You're not *that* ugly. Some lad will go for you one day, I'll bet."

Nell laughed out loud. "Well, thank you . . . I think," she said, "but it's not that easy for royals. We've got to marry other royals, you see. We can't always marry someone we love. Love potions make life more . . . bearable."

"Zow," said Owen. "That ronks. Doesn't that bother you?"

Nell shrugged. "It's just the way it is," she said. "I've never given it much thought."

"Well, you ought to," said Owen.

"Why?" said Nell. "I can't change it."

"Why not?" asked Owen.

"Because I have a duty to fulfill," said Nell.

"Well, I'll tell you something," said Owen. "I thought it was tough livin' in the Lanes, but I'd rather live in the Lanes forever than have to marry someone I could only stand by taking a love potion."

Nell frowned. "It must be nice to have only yourself to worry about," she said shortly. "We royals have . . . higher obligations."

"That so?" said Owen. "I think maybe you've just got higher opinions of yourselves. What would be so terrible about a royal marrying an ordinary person? Someone like me, for instance? What makes you better than me?"

"I . . . well, I . . . ," Nell stammered, flustered by Owen's words. "I don't know. I mean, I *don't* think I'm better than you. I just . . . oh . . ."

"I'll tell you what I think," said Owen. "I think you royals marry one another to keep all the coin in the family."

"That's not true!" cried Nell.

"No?" asked Owen. "Then how is it you all live so rich and fancy while the lot of us in the Lanes live like beggars? I'll bet you don't even know how it feels to be hungry."

Nell swallowed uncomfortably. "Look," she said. "I don't have time for this right now. I have too many other things to worry about. I really have to go."

She was about to douse the speaking star when she noticed a dark mound on the corner of Owen's desk.

"Is that a cat?" she asked.

"A what?" asked Owen.

"A cat. Is that a cat on the corner of the desk?"

"Oh. Um . . . no." Owen turned slowly so Nell could see the back of his head. "It's your hair."

"My hair?" cried Nell. "Put it back on! What if someone walks in?"

"Well, they sort of already know," said Owen.

"Already know!" cried Nell. "What do you mean?"

"I mean I . . . that is . . . you . . . gave yourself a haircut."

"A what!?"

"I'm sorry," said Owen. "I just couldn't stand that thing hangin' down my back all day like a big old, itchy tail. I took it off and told them I'd cut it."

"By the Scepter of Light!" cried Nell. "What happened?"

"Well, Madame S. made a big puss-face and said she was going to have to 'report this to the king'! So, I guess you might be in a bit of trouble when you get home."

Nell sighed heavily. "Thanks," she quipped. "That's *all* I need."

"Which reminds me, you haven't told me how *you* are yet," said Owen. "Is everything all right?"

"What do you care?" Nell snapped.

"I . . . care," said Owen clumsily. "You may be a stuck-up snob at times, but other times . . . well, I just care, okay?"

The brusqueness in Owen's voice couldn't mask an underlying sincerity that brought quick tears to Nell's eyes. For a moment she was tempted to tell him how cold and lonely and frightened she was. But that wouldn't be wise. It would just prompt more questions. She brushed her tears away.

"I'm fine," she said quietly. "I'll check in with you again as soon as I can."

"All right," said Owen. "You watch yourself, hear?"

"I will. And *you* stay out of trouble!"

"I'll try," said Owen. "Good-bye."

"Bye Owen."

The star went dark, and Nell sat staring at it for a long moment. How she wished she was back home, back with her father, and Lady Fidelia, and . . . yes, even Owen. Troublesome as he was, she was growing fond of him. When this was all over . . . if . . . if things turned out all right, maybe they could be friends. Maybe she could find him a position at court. But no . . . Owen wanted to go to Wizard University, and she had promised to help him. A promise was a promise.

Nell tucked the speaking star safely away, pulled out her vanishroud, and bunched it into a pillow. With a tired sigh, she lay down, pulled Minna close, and closed her eyes.

CHAPTER EIGHTEEN

Nell woke shrieking. Something was slithering across her face! She sat up, frantically clawing at herself. Everywhere she touched, slimy creatures clung to her clothes and skin.

"Rrronk!" cried Minna, wakened by Nell's screams.

"Flame, Minna, flame!" Nell cried.

Obediently, Minna exhaled a stream of flame.

By the flare of light, Nell looked around. The floor and walls of the cave were seething with wretched, writhing vermin.

"Let's get out of here!" she screamed.

She shoved her shroud into its pouch then jumped from the ledge. Oozy things squished beneath her feet. She slipped, going down on her knees in the living sludge.

"Aach!" she cried, shivering with revulsion as she jumped to her feet once more.

Minna hovered nervously.

"This way!" Nell cried, wading ankle-deep through the slithering sea.

At last she reached the mouth of the dark passageway.

"Flame, Minna," she called again, her heart still pounding.

Minna obliged, illuminating a narrow earthen corridor with an abundance of hairy, rootlike growths hanging down from its ceiling. A few crawly creatures slithered away from the light, but nothing like the numbers behind her. Nell hurried into the passageway, brushing the roots aside as she walked. After a while she slowed her steps and breathed a sigh of relief, suddenly realizing how hungry and thirsty she was.

"I'll bet you're hungry and thirsty too, aren't you Minna?" she said. "As soon as we get out of this passageway, I'll give you some water."

"Thrummm," said Minna.

Nell felt a small pinch and something tugged at her arm. One of the roots had snagged her sleeve. She tugged at it, but it had burrowed into the cloth like a burr. Then there was another pinch on her other arm. Another root.

"Minna," she called. "Flame."

Minna opened her mouth and another burst of flame shot out. By the light Nell could see that rootlike suckers had begun curling out from the cave walls, all reaching for her!

"Flame, Minna, flame!" she cried, pointing to the root that held fast to her right arm.

Minna aimed a stream of flame at the sucker until it frizzled and let go, but now Nell's left arm was bound fast. More roots were curling around both her legs and another was snaking around her neck! She tugged at them in a panic.

"Hurry, Minna!" she cried.

Minna darted from root to root, spraying flame, but the roots were growing faster than she could stop them. Nell would be trapped like an insect in a web if she didn't do something fast. But what?

"Owen's dagger!" she whispered.

With her free hand she reached beneath her skirts and pulled the dagger from its sheath just as another sucker latched onto her right shoulder. She slipped the dagger between her neck and the vine. There was a flare of light and the vine fell away. Quickly she slashed away the other suckers, but by now the passageway ahead was filling with vines.

"Hurry, Minna!" Nell cried. "We've got to get out of here!"

She cut and slashed at the suckers. By her side Minna fought bravely, belching flames. Slowly, inch-by-inch they battled their way through the twisted maze until Nell was dizzy with exhaustion. She feared that she might faint at any moment when finally she caught a pale glimmer of light filtering through the tangled mass.

"We must be getting close to the end!" Nell cried, her chest heaving. "Keep fighting, Minna!"

Soon Nell could smell fresh air and feel a bit of a breeze on her sweaty brow. She rounded a corner and saw a bright shaft of daylight, but even as she struggled toward it, roots began to fill it in!

"Hurry, Minna!" she cried, slashing wildly. By the time she reached the opening, it was barely large enough to squeeze through. She pushed Minna ahead of her, hacked her leg free of the last vine, and wriggled out, tumbling down an embankment to a small ledge. She lay there trembling with fear and fatigue.

Minna settled down beside her, wheezing.

"You okay?" Nell asked.

"Thrummm," said Minna tiredly.

Nell rubbed Minna's nubby head affectionately. She looked back up the mountainside, but if the passage was still there its opening was lost in the tangle of brush.

"Thanks, little friend," she said to Minna. "I don't think I'd have made it without you." Then she held up the dagger. "Or without Owen," she added. She tucked the knife back into her pouch, then took out her water-skin and gave Minna a drink. The little Dragon gulped and gulped. Nell licked her lips enviously, her own mouth dry as dust. This quest was harder than she'd ever imagined. How much more would she have to endure?

Nell looked around her and found herself high up on a mountainside, the sky above shimmering through strange, watery clouds. The air was warm, for which she was grateful, but the thick humidity wasn't helping her still-damp clothes.

More mountains stretched off to the north and south, curving around like great arms to encircle a bowl-shape valley. On the western side a narrow gorge split the valley, like a crack in the bowl. There was no green vegetation anywhere, only shades of gray and blue. Snaking down the center of the valley, a river glinted silver in the pale sunlight. It was all very lovely, in a cold, metallic sort of way.

A faintly visible footpath zigzagged down toward the valley floor. It was overgrown with weeds and brambles and littered with rocks and boulders from countless landslides.

"Doesn't look like they get much foot traffic around here," Nell mumbled.

Minna ventured off on short hunting expeditions as Nell began her descent. The demi returned frequently, offering to share an assortment of grapes, nuts, and berries, but despite her gnawing hunger, Nell had no choice but to refuse.

Rocks rolled and slipped beneath her feet, and she fell often, tearing her clothes and scraping her legs. The air grew warmer and steamier the lower she went, and soon she was drenched in sweat and covered in layers of grime. She stopped to catch her breath and the valley swam before her eyes. She put a hand to her head, waiting for the whirling to stop.

"I'm getting so dizzy," she mumbled. "I don't know how much longer I can go on without food."

Just then Minna returned from one of her little foraging trips in a state of exhilaration.

"Thrummm," she kept singing. "Thrummm, thrummm!"

"What are you so cheerful about?" Nell asked.

Minna dove and returned, dove and returned, entreating Nell to follow.

"I'm coming as quickly as I can," said Nell. "*Some* of us don't have wings, you know."

Minna stared down into the valley, her tail switching eagerly.

Nell strained to see what had Minna so enthused. After climbing a bit lower, she began to pick out buildings. A village! But what kind? She had no idea who inhabited these lands. She continued her descent cautiously until she saw what Minna was so excited about. One of the outlying buildings had a number of great cages surrounding it.

"Dragons, Minna!" she cried. "There are Dragons down there!"

"Thrummm," sang Minna.

Just at that moment Nell heard a scrabbling sound behind her. She whirled around, but it was too late. A heavy cloth dropped over her head. Before she could move, it was cinched in around her waist and again about her knees. Her arms were pinned helplessly to her sides.

"Who's there?" Nell cried. "What do you want?"

No one answered.

"Rrronk!" Minna cried. "Rrronk!" Her voice faded in and out along with the ashy smell of firebreath. The little Dragon was trying to drive the intruder off.

There came a loud whistle, then the clop of hooves. Nell felt herself lifted off the ground and tossed sacklike across an animal's broad back.

"ZZsss, zzsss," Minna hissed, her breath close by Nell's ear.

"Get out of here, worm!" a gruff voice shouted.

There was a slap, a small cry, and the desperate flapping of wings.

"Minna, no!" Nell cried. "Stay away!"

Minna began shrieking again, but from a distance.

"Ouch!" Nell cried as more bindings tightened around her, lashing her to the pack animal. "Let me go!" She kicked and struggled to no avail.

The pack animal began to move, its broad body shifting from side to side as its hooves thudded against the rocky cliffs. There were other shuffling footsteps, too, and an occasional grunt.

"Who are you?" Nell cried repeatedly.

There was no reply.

The dusty blanket was stifling, and the ropes cut painfully into Nell's wrists and legs with the animal's every swaying step.

"Please," Nell begged. "Whoever you are, let me down."

Still no reply.

At long last the beast came to a halt. A knife sliced into Nell's bindings and she tumbled to the ground, whacking her head painfully on a rock. Slowly she flexed her arms and legs. Ouch! They ached, but they seemed to work. Her ribs hurt and there was an aching lump on her forehead, but nothing seemed broken.

There came a soft thump on her chest and little claws scratched at the cloth that still covered her body.

"Out of here, worm!" someone shouted again, and then Nell heard Minna give a shriek of pain.

"Leave her alone!" Nell cried.

Rough hands tore her wrappings away and Nell sat up, blinking at the sudden brightness. Leaning over her, silhouetted against the sky was a thickset man with a pointed head and long, hairy arms.

"What . . . what are you?" asked Nell hesitantly.

"I be a Trog," said the man. "And yer a trespasser."

"I'm sorry," said Nell. "I'm just trying to get across the valley. I don't mean any harm."

"Aar," said the Trog, growling. "That be what them all says." He was fearsomely dressed, with spiked leather armor and a sword at his waist. He bent low and grabbed Nell's arm, eyeing her curiously. "Ya be a female," he said.

"Yes," said Nell, yanking her arm away. Then she heard a small, shuddering gasp. She turned to see Minna lying in the dirt a few feet away.

"Minna!" she shrieked. "What have you done to Minna, you brute?" She began kicking and flailing at the Trog. He let out a deep, throaty chuckle.

"Fiesty one arn't ya," he said, holding her at arms' length. "Don't worry. Yer worm arn't hurt. Just got the wind knocked out of her is all."

The Trog picked Minna up by the tail and dropped her into Nell's lap. After a few additional gasps, Minna began to breathe more regularly. Nell hugged her close and glared at the Trog.

"You're nothing but a coward," she said, "hitting a little creature like this." Her hand slipped beneath the folds of her skirt and closed around the hilt of the dagger.

The Trog started to laugh. "And yer a bold little snip," he said. "I likes yer spunk. I was goin' to feed ya to me Dragons, but I think maybe I'll keep ya."

"Keep me?" cried Nell.

"Aar," said the Trog. "Come now. Here be a hand up."

Hesitantly, Nell let go of the dagger and took hold of the great, hairy hand. The Trog pulled her to her feet.

"You can't *keep* me," said Nell. "I don't belong to you."

The Trog chortled. "Ya don't eh? Where be yer man, then?"

Nell stared up at him. "I don't have a man," she said.

The Trog scratched his head. "Then who looks after ya?" he asked.

"I look after myself, thank you," said Nell.

The Trog snorted. "From the looks of ya, yer not doing so good."

Nell looked down at her filthy, ragged clothes and her dirt-caked arms and legs.

"I just need a bath is all," she said. "I've been traveling for some time."

"Aar," said the Trog. "Well, come along. I thinks I'll give ya to me missus. Her'll be glad of another slave."

"Another slave!" cried Nell.

"Aar," said the Trog. "Her only has one."

Nell stared up at the fierce, hairy man in horror. "But you can't . . . I mean, you don't . . . ," she stammered.

"Can't what?" asked the Trog. "Keep ya?" He looked around. "Don't see no one ta stop me, do ya?"

Nell cleared her throat. "Please," she said. "I don't know much about housework and such. I wouldn't make a very good slave. Besides, I really must be going."

The Trog chuckled again. "Ya be a funny one," he said. "The missus are gonna love ya!"

"No, I can't–," Nell began, but the Trog suddenly seemed to lose all his good humor.

"Ya'll do what I say, ya hear?" he boomed, glaring at Nell. "Er I change me mind and chop ya into fodder!"

Minna whimpered in Nell's arms.

"Y-Yes, sir," said Nell.

"That be better," said the Trog. "Step lively, then."

Chapter Nineteen

The Trog village was a maze of walled-in courtyards. The Trog led Nell through the gate of the closest one, the one with the Dragon cages out back. Inside was a small house made of sticks and mud. It resembled a stack of boxes, with a rickety chimney protruding from the lowest box, belching blue smoke into the sky. Beyond the wall, Nell could see dozens of other house-tops with similar plumes of smoke drifting skyward.

The Trog pushed his front door open and motioned Nell through. Inside, it took a moment for her eyes to adjust to the dimness, then she looked around. The room was small but clean, with simple wooden furniture and bare floors. Intricately knotted wall hangings and several finely woven baskets gave Nell hope, as did a clay vase filled with flowers in the center of the table. If Trogs loved beauty, they couldn't be all bad.

A slightly less hairy Trog was seated in a chair, nursing a baby, while a little toddler played by her feet.

Near the hearth, a young girl stirred a great tub of steaming laundry.

"Leah," shouted the Trog to the nursing woman. "Look what I brung ya."

The woman looked at Nell with a puzzled expression. "What?" she said. "What be that?"

"It be another slave," said the man.

"That dirty little snip of a thing?" said Leah. "Why, her be but a child!"

"Her be a slave now ya ungrateful wench," the man snarled. "And if ya don't watch yer step, I'll sell ya to the Kwarts and yer'll be one, too."

Leah's eyes narrowed, but she said nothing more.

The Trog gave Nell a push. "Get on over ther and help Talitha," he said, pointing to the girl at the tub.

Nell started forward, but the Trog grabbed her back. "Not so fast," he growled, pulling Minna from her arms. "The worm comes with me."

"Rrronk!" cried Minna, digging into his hand until her claws drew blood.

"Argh!" he cried, shaking her loose.

She darted up to the rafters just as a gong sounded somewhere outside.

"The war council," said Leah. "Ya'd better go."

The Trog looked up and shook his fist at Minna. "I'll get you later," he barked, then he turned and stalked out of the door.

"Come, Minna," said Nell.

Minna zoomed down into her arms and Nell stroked

her ruffled scales. "There now," she whispered. "I won't let him hurt you again."

Leah, the Trog's "missus," eyed the two of them curiously.

"Ya got a name?" she asked.

"Nell," said Nell.

Leah nodded at Minna. "That worm housebroken?"

"Yes," said Nell.

Leah said something else, but her toddler had started whining, and it was hard to hear. Nell spied a ball lying beneath the table. "Look, Minna," she said, pointing to it. "Why don't you play with the little boy?"

With a joyful cry, Minna scooped up the ball. Then she flew over and dropped it at the child's feet. Delighted, the child picked it up and tossed it. Soon Minna was zipping around the room with the toddler in giggly pursuit.

Leah smiled in appreciation. She burped the baby, a little girl, and put it on her shoulder, then she spoke again, in a softer tone.

"What manner of creature are ya?" she asked.

"I'm one of the Tallfolk," said Nell.

"Ya don't look so tall ta me," said Leah. "Where are ya from?"

"From the kingdom of Xandria," said Nell, "beyond the mountains. I came through the waterfall."

Leah arched an eyebrow, then she turned and winked at the girl stirring the laundry tub. "Got us a dreamer here," she said.

"I'm not a dreamer," said Nell. "It's true."

Talitha laughed. "How is it yer out without yer man?" she asked.

"I don't have a man," said Nell, "unless you mean my father. I . . . sort of *tricked* him."

Talitha's eyes lit up. "Aar?" she said. "I'd like ta know how."

"I dressed a boy up to look like me and take my place," said Nell. "Then I ran off."

Leah's mouth dropped. "Yer having us on," she said.

"I'm not," said Nell.

Leah shook her head in disbelief. "Things must be far different in this dreamworld of yers," she said. "Yer'd never get away with that here in Cerulea."

"It took some doing," said Nell, "but I managed."

Leah smiled wistfully. "Would that us could get free of Orson so easy, eh, Talitha?" she said.

Nell was surprised to hear Leah speaking so congenially to the slave girl.

"Who is Orson?" she asked the two women.

"Him what brought ya here," said Leah. "Me husband."

"You mean, you aren't happy with him?" Nell asked.

"Happy?" Leah laughed. She got up and tucked her sleeping baby into a little cradle near the hearth, then she straightened and stared at the child sadly. "What woman is happy?" she asked quietly. "'Tis a curse to be born female."

"In Xandria women are happy," said Nell. Then she

remembered the harrowed faces she had seen in the Lanes. "At least, most of them are," she added.

Leah looked over her shoulder at Nell. "Don't men be cruel ther?" she asked.

"Some," said Nell. "But most are good and kind, especially to their wives and children."

Leah turned. "Be ther no war camps?" she asked.

"War camps?" Nell shrugged. "I'm not sure what you mean."

"Camps where them takes the boys once them reach ther tweens," said Leah. "Where them be taught ta hate and kill. Where all the love be beat out of them."

Nell frowned and shook her head. "I know of nothing like that," she said. "There are camps where young men are trained as soldiers, but they aren't . . ."

Leah listened intently as Nell described the military camps of Xandria, her eyes growing wistful. "Would that the war camps here were such," she said. "Maybe then Orson'd yet be the gentle boy him was when we was young."

"You knew him as a child?" Nell asked.

"Aar," said Leah. "Him and me older brother was friends and him came often ta visit. Him told me stories and brung me treats and trinkets. Him were so kind, I grew ta love him, even though we was both but children."

"But, surely that kind boy must still be inside Orson somewhere," said Nell.

"Hah!" Talitha lifted a coarsely woven shirt from the tub and twisted the water from it. "Don't make us laugh," she said with a scowl. "Orson don't have a gentle bone left in him's body."

Leah sighed heavily. "Aar," she said. "Talitha be right. I think it be the gentlest ones that the camps scar the worst. Though now and then I think I catches a glimmer of *something* in Orson's eye when him looks at the children. . . ."

"Don't fool yerself, Leah," Talitha cautioned. "All yer seein' is what ya long ta see. Orson'd sell the lot of us fer a pint of joy juice if him took the notion."

Leah pressed her lips into a thin line of resignation and nodded. "Aar, ya speak the truth, Talitha," she said with a sigh, then she sucked in a deep breath and squared her shoulders. "Yer'd best take Nell out and teach her her duties now. I'll finish up ther washin'. Take little Raja along with ya."

"No!" Nell interrupted. "*Please.* You don't understand. I really *can't* stay here. You've got to let me go."

Leah shook her head. "Ya be a daft little thing," she said, "but I likes yer heart. I'd let ya go if I could, but Orson would bash me purple. Now off with ya, and pay attention. If ya don't do yer chores right, it'll be you that gets bashed."

CHAPTER TWENTY

Talitha motioned to the toddler.

"Come, Raja," she said. "Go see Dragons."

"'Ragons," squealed the child, running over and grabbing Talitha's hand.

"Come," the slave girl said to Nell.

With a sigh of resignation, Nell called Minna to follow and trudged out the door after Talitha.

They walked around the house to the barns and cages. The Dragons, many of whom had been sleeping, woke now and began pacing and bellowing. They were terrible-looking, but beautiful, too, though not so multi-colored as the Dragons Nell was used to seeing. Like everything else in this place, they were mainly blue with shades of purple and gray.

"Why are they so fierce-looking?" Nell asked.

"Them're fighters," said Talitha. "Orson traps them in the hills and trains them for the pits."

The pits! Nell shivered. Was that what Orson had in mind to do with Minna?

"How did you come to be his slave?" asked Nell.

"I were captured in the war," Talitha replied.

"What war?" asked Nell.

"Just the war," said Talitha. "That's all us calls it. It be between us Kwarts and the Trogs. It been going on so long us can't remember a time without it."

Nell stared at Talitha in disbelief.

"Why?" she asked. "What is it about?"

Talitha sighed. "In the beginning," she said, "Kwarts sided with Galerinn and Trogs with Graieconn. When the Great War ended, the hate didn't, so Kwarts and Trogs just kept on fighting."

"All these centuries?" said Nell.

"Aar," said Talitha sadly. "All these centuries."

"Leah doesn't treat you like a slave," Nell observed. "Why?"

"Us women be tired of war," said Talitha. "Us kill them. Them kill us. It haves no end. I growed up thinking Trogs was horrible monsters what would kill and eat the Kwarts if them could. But Trogs be no different from Kwarts. The men is all just as stubborn and fierce, living for them's blood games and them's war. And the women is all just as sad, raising them's little boys to be taught to hate and kill; raising them's little girls to be slaves, whether captured in war or married off. It be much the same here."

They had arrived at the barn where the feed was

kept—great bins filled with a mix of mashed grains, fire-weed, and raw meat. Talitha put Raja in a small pen with some toys, and Nell asked Minna to stay and keep him company. Then Talitha rolled out a large cart. She handed Nell a shovel and grabbed one for herself and the two began shoveling feed.

"If all the women feel the way you do," said Nell, "why don't you get together and do something about it?"

"Us can't get together," said Talitha. "Women don't be allowed out of them's compounds, don't be allowed to speak to other women, except for them's slaves."

Nell shoveled and shoveled, pondering Talitha's words.

"Maybe I can help you," she said at last.

"Help us? How?" asked Talitha.

"I'm going to see the Imperial Wizard," said Nell.

Talitha snorted. "Fat lot'a good that'll do," she said.

"But the Imperial Wizard maintains the balance," said Nell. "He sees to it that evil never oughtweighs good in the world."

Talitha snorted again and tossed a last shovel of feed into the cart. "Not in *this* world," she said.

She grabbed the handles of the cart and steered it toward the door.

Nell ran after her.

"But I *can* help," she said. "I'm going to be the Imperial Wizard's apprentice."

At this Talitha stopped pushing and stared at Nell.

"Yer is the daftest little thing I've ever met," she said

with a smile. "It will be amusing, having ya about."

"But I *can't* stay," said Nell. "I must reach the Imperial Wizard by tomorrow night!"

"Aar," said Talitha, winking. "Well, come along. Ya'd best hurry and get yer work done then."

She rolled the cart up to the first cage and showed Nell how to shovel the feed through a slot into a trough on the other side of the cage bars. The Dragons began nipping and clawing at one another, fighting to be near the trough.

"Easy now, easy," soothed Talitha as she moved to the next slot.

There was a lid covering each trough, and Talitha told Nell that these were to remain closed until all the troughs in the cage were full.

"Else the stronger Dragons will just follow ya from trough to trough," she explained, "eating the food as fast as ya shovel it and leaving nothing fer the smaller ones."

Once all the troughs in the first cage were filled, Talitha pulled on a chain. It went through a pulley suspended high above the cage and connected to a web of other chains, each linked to one of the lids. In an instant all the troughs were opened, and the Dragons rushed to feed.

As she watched them, an idea began to take form in Nell's head.

"Talitha," she said suddenly. "What about the Dragons?"

"What?" asked Talitha.

"The Dragons," said Nell. "Let me take one and fly out of here before Orson returns. I can tie you up and you can pretend I overpowered you."

Talitha shook her head and smiled. "Ya just doesn't give up, does ya?" she said.

"No," said Nell. "I can't. My quest is too important."

Talitha laughed good-naturedly.

"Well," she said, "even if I was of a mind to get meself killed for letting ya steal one of Orson's Dragons, it wouldn't do ya no good. Thems for the pits, like I told ya. Them's wings is clipped."

Nell's heart sank.

"Except . . . ," Talitha added thoughtfully.

"Except what?" asked Nell.

"Nar," said Talitha, shaking her head. "Her's too sick anyway."

"Who's too sick?" asked Nell.

"The albino," said Talitha. "Him caught her last week. Her just be a yearling, but them others has been so hard on her—biting her and scorching her and such . . ."

"What others?" asked Nell.

"Them other Dragons," said Talitha. "Them pick on her because her's different. Her's so beaten up and weak that Orson can't use her. Him's got her in the slaughter cage out back. Him's going to chop her into feed."

Nell's stomach lurched. "The poor thing," she said. "Can I see her?"

"Us has other cages to finish first," said Talitha.

When the last of the great Dragons had been fed, Talitha filled a small bucket with food and handed it to Nell. "Her probably won't touch it," she said, "but bring it just in case." Then she picked up Raja.

"Come on," she said. "Go see Albino."

"'Bino," repeated the child, pointing toward the door.

"Come, Minna," said Nell.

Minna flew to her shoulder, and Nell followed Talitha out of the barn and around to the back. There, huddled in the corner of a small cage, was the sorriest-looking Dragon Nell had ever seen. It sat with its head lolling listlessly, staring glassy-eyed at nothing. Its scales were a dull, dead-looking white, and its scrawny body was covered with scorches and raw patches where scales were missing.

"Rrronk," cried Minna when she saw it.

Nell's heart broke. She walked over to the cage and reached her fingers through, longing to touch the poor beast, to stroke it the way she stroked Minna whenever Minna was frightened or hurt.

"Poor beauty," she whispered.

Slowly, the creature swung its head in her direction, gazing at her with sad, lavender eyes.

"Come, beauty," said Nell gently. "Let me touch you."

The creature continued to stare, but did not move.

Nell turned to Talitha.

"Can I bring the food in to her?" she asked.

Talitha shrugged. "Suit yerself," she said. She went over and lifted the latch.

Slowly, carefully, Nell inched through the door, trying hard not to startle the creature, murmuring gentle words. The creature's eyes followed her every move and when Nell stepped forward, it shuddered, but it didn't move.

"Are you hungry?" Nell asked, holding out the bucket so the creature could see what it held.

It took no interest.

Suddenly Minna flew through the door and zipped over to hover just in front of the beast's nose. It stared at her curiously.

"Thrummm," said Minna softly, then she nuzzled the creature.

The Dragon pulled back and blinked its eyes. Minna nuzzled it again, turned around and came back and nuzzled Nell's nose.

Nell smiled and nuzzled her in return.

Minna did this three more times, back and forth and back and forth, until at last the beast nuzzled her in return, ever so gently.

"Thrummm," sang Minna.

"Grrrummm," rumbled the beast.

"Well, I'll be," whispered Talitha. "That be ther first spark of life I've seen in her."

Nell stepped forward, cautiously. The beast watched her, but did not move. When Nell was close enough, she set the bucket down, then reached out very slowly and stroked the creature's neck.

"There," she whispered. "There, there, beauty."

The creature stared into Nell's eyes, and Nell sent it mental pictures of love and warmth and caring.

"I'm going to name you Beauty because that's what you are," she said, stroking the creature's nose now. "Minna and I are going to take care of you. We're going to help you get well."

Then, to Nell's amazement, the Dragon lowered its head to the bucket and began to feed.

CHAPTER TWENTY-ONE

Nell turned to Talitha.

"Can I take her?" she asked.

Talitha was still staring at the Dragon in disbelief. She turned to Nell and slowly shook her head.

"Nar," she said. "It's clear her should be yers, and I wish I could give her to ya, but Orson'll fly into a rage if him finds one of him's Dragons gone—even this one—and him's rage is a terrible thing."

Nell sighed. She felt her drawstring pouch through her skirts, toying with the idea of stealing the Dragon by force. But she couldn't bring herself to pull the dagger on Talitha. Besides, how could she leave Talitha and Leah and the children to face Orson's wrath? She let go of the pouch.

"That's it!" she cried suddenly.

Talitha looked at her.

"Are you serious about wanting to leave here?" Nell asked.

Talitha didn't hesitate. "Of course," she said.

"And Leah? Would she really go?"

"Aar," said Talitha. "Her dreams of a better life for her little ones, but if yer thinking us can all fly out of here on this broken-down beast . . ."

"No," said Nell, "that's not what I'm thinking. This is what I'm thinking." She reached under her skirt and pulled her shroud from the pouch. Then she tossed it over her head.

"What the . . . ? Where is ya?" cried Talitha.

"Right here," said Nell, lifting the shroud slowly.

"Wha . . . how did ya do that?" Talitha asked.

"It's a vanishroud," said Nell. "You can put it on and move about without being seen. You and Leah can sneak the babies right out of this village. You could even come back and get some of the other women if you wanted to."

Talitha stared at her openmouthed.

"But . . . where would us go?" she asked.

"I don't know," said Nell. "That's up to you. What lies beyond that gorge?" She pointed to the west.

"Don't know," said Talitha. "That gorge be Droog territory. Kwarts and Trogs don't go there."

"Well, the Droogs won't see you if you're wearing the shroud," said Nell.

Talitha still looked uncertain.

"Look," Nell said. "Maybe you don't know what lies beyond that gorge, but you sure enough know what life will be like if you stay here. Is it what you want?"

Talitha chewed her lip thoughtfully for a long moment, then she nodded and a light came into her eyes. "Yer right," she said, reaching for the shroud. "Take yer Dragon and go, quickly, before *him* gets back."

Nell grinned. "Thank you, Talitha," she said. "I know you don't believe me, but I really *am* going to see the Imperial Wizard, and I really will help you one day if I can."

"Aar," said Talitha, smiling warmly. "I don't doubt ya will, ya daft little thing."

Nell gently fastened a Dragon halter around Beauty's neck, then led her out of the cage. She rubbed the slender nose gently and spoke in soft tones.

"I'm about to ask a lot of you," she said. "You're tired and weak and sick, but we have to get out of here. I need you to let me ride on your back. We need to fly." She held the image in her mind until she saw the light of understanding in the creature's eyes.

Ever so gently, talking quietly the whole time, Nell began to climb up Beauty's tail, up her back, to the spot between her shoulder blades that formed a natural seat. Beauty did not object. Obviously she had grasped the mental pictures, because when Nell sat down and took hold of the reins, Beauty automatically lifted her wings.

"That's it!" cried Nell. "That's my Beauty!"

"Thrummm," sang Minna.

"Lead the way, Minna!" Nell cried. "Up there! Out of this valley!"

Minna sprang into the air, and Nell tugged on the reins, signaling Beauty to follow.

"Away!" she cried, giving the traditional signal for a Dragon to mount to the sky.

Beauty crouched and then sprang, but she was so weak that she merely fluttered along the ground a few cubits and then crashed in an exhausted heap.

"Oh, Beauty," said Nell sadly. "I'm so sorry to ask this of you, but you've got to keep trying. Please." She tugged gently on the reins once again.

Beauty struggled to her feet. With an enormous effort she crouched, sprang, then raked at the air with her wings.

And then they were airborne!

"Yes, Beauty!" Nell encouraged. "You're doing it!"

Slowly they climbed up, up, into the mountains, Beauty's great wings rising and falling, Minna fluttering madly to keep up. Gradually the valley fell away and then they were flying through the strange, watery clouds. At last they burst through into clear sky. Instinctively Nell turned Beauty toward the sun. They sailed between two snow-capped peaks. Below them mounds of brown hills stepped down to meet a broad golden plain that stretched far, far into the distance toward another snow-capped mountain chain. The air was delightfully cool and dry with the pale yellow sun hanging low over the faroff mountains. Here and there Nell saw clusters of small tents or hovels, but Nell had no idea who inhabited them, and after her experience in Cerulea, no wish to find out.

Beauty was wheezing badly, her sides heaving.

"Just a little farther, girl," Nell urged.

In time the mountain shadow began crawling across the plain, and Nell realized night would soon follow. She searched the plain below for a likely place to make camp.

By now Beauty's sides were heaving so badly that Nell was afraid her heart might burst. At last, below on the ground, Nell saw what she'd been hoping for: a small lake.

"There, Beauty," she said, tugging the reigns. "Down."

Beauty spiraled down and landed roughly on the banks of the lake. Then she crumpled in exhaustion. Nell quickly slid from her back and dropped to her knees by the water.

With a cry of joy, Minna dove out of the sky straight into the lake.

Nell cupped her hand, dipped it into the lake, and took a small sip of water. It tasted so cool and fresh sliding down her parched throat that she was tempted to gulp huge quantities. She knew she couldn't, though. Instead she filled her waterskin and poured it into Beauty's gasping mouth.

Beauty sputtered and coughed, then finally swallowed. Over and over Nell filled the waterskin until Beauty's thirst was slaked. Then she filled it again and gently washed and cooled Beauty until at last the heaving stopped and the young Dragon fell asleep.

Minna was still splashing delightedly in the lake.

"My, that looks refreshing," said Nell. She cast about for signs of danger, but the whole area seemed deserted. Satisfied that they were safe for the time being, she stripped off her clothes and waded in.

The water felt so cool, so fresh. She dove under, letting it swish through her hair and ripple over her body. She rolled and twirled and tumbled, giggling like a little girl again. How long it seemed since she had felt so carefree. How good it felt to be rid of those layers of sweat and grime!

But night was falling and the campsite needed securing. Reluctantly Nell climbed out at last, wringing the water from her hair. She shivered in the evening chill.

"We need to make a fire to keep us warm, Minna," she said, "and to ward off wild creatures."

She stared into the gathering gloom and shivered. Were there Night Things here, she wondered? She looked at Beauty, still sleeping deeply by the lake's edge. The Dragon had the lake at her back. If Nell built the fire in front of her, Beauty would be fairly safe. As safe as any of them.

Too tired and hungry to gather firewood, Nell began pointing her finger at assorted sticks and scraps of brush. One by one they rose and flew through the air to land at her feet. When there was a decent pile, she called Minna.

"Flame, Minna," she said.

Whoosh!

Minna breathed out fire until the sticks caught and blazed.

"Good girl," said Nell. "Now, you'd better go find yourself some supper before it's fully dark."

Obediently Minna fluttered off and Nell looked down at her pile of filthy clothes. How she wished she had Lady Fidelia's wand. . . . But she didn't. With a tired sigh she returned to the lake's edge and scrubbed the grubby garments as best she could. She twisted the excess water out of them, then stretched them out on stick frames in front of the fire. She spied a stubby log a short distance away.

"Roll," she said, guiding it over to the fireside. Wearily she plopped down on the makeshift seat and pulled her speaking star from its pouch. The crackling fire felt good. The temperature had dropped dramatically with the setting of the sun.

"Owen," she said, "at the academy."

Slowly the star began to glow, and then Owen's form wavered in the center. But why was the image so dim tonight?

"Owen?" said Nell.

Owen looked up. "Nell?" he said. "Where are you?"

"I'm here," said Nell. "You can't see me, remember?"

"Sure wish I could," said Owen with a sigh.

Nell looked at her drying clothes and giggled.

"Good thing you can't," she said.

"Why?" asked Owen.

"Never mind," said Nell. "I can hardly even see you. Why is it so dark there tonight?"

"Well . . . I'm sort of . . . in the dungeon," said Owen.

Nell's eyes flew wide. "The what!?" she cried, shrieking.

"Now, calm down," said Owen. "It's just for tonight. It's not that bad, really. I mean, there aren't any rats or anything."

Nell groaned. "What are you doing in the dungeon?" she asked.

"Well . . . I . . . that is . . . you . . . or . . . we . . ."

"Get to the point!" Nell barked.

"I'm getting to it, I'm getting to it."

"I'm waiting," said Nell impatiently.

"Well, we had potions lab today," said Owen, "and we were supposed to try out mixing up those love potions that we learned last night."

"Go on," said Nell.

"Well I mixed mine up," said Owen, "and I tried it out on a couple of rats like I was supposed to."

"Yes?" said Nell.

"And it worked great," said Owen. "I mean, you should've seen those lovey-doveys. It was embarrassing." He chuckled.

"I'm not amused, Owen," said Nell.

"Right." Owen cleared his throat. "Well, it worked *so* good," he went on, "that I was dying to see how it would work on a person."

"Oh, no." Nell groaned. "*Who* did you try it on?"

"Um . . . Madame Sofia."

"What!?"

"Well, she was sitting right next to me at lunch and her tea cup was right there, and the vial was right in my pocket, and the next thing I knew I was just sort of . . ."

"Putting the love potion in her tea!?" shrieked Nell.

"Yeah," said Owen. "That's pretty much it."

Nell groaned again.

"What happened next?" she asked.

"Well, Madame Sofia was talking to this crabby old Wizard on the other side of her. He teaches Incantations and he smells like . . . like I used to, actually. Only about five times worse."

"Eeew," said Nell.

"Anyway," Owen went on, "Madame S. reached for her cup and took a big swig of tea, and the next thing you know, she was all over the guy! It took half the faculty to pull her away from him."

In spite of herself, Nell burst out giggling.

Owen started laughing too. "It *was* pretty funny," he said between chuckles. "Mmmwah, mmmwah, mmmwah. She just kept planting these big wet smackers all over him. The whole school was going crazy."

Nell groaned. "Oh, Owen," she said. "What am I going to do with you?"

"Funny," said Owen, "that's the same thing Madame S. said when the potion wore off. Then she said, 'Princess or not, you'll have to spend the night in the dungeon.'"

"Well, it serves you right," said Nell. "Do you think you can possibly stay out of trouble tomorrow?"

"I'll try," said Owen.

"Try *hard*," said Nell. "I have enough things to worry about right now."

"Like what?" asked Owen.

"Never mind," said Nell. "I've got to go. I'll check in with you tomorrow."

"Wait!" said Owen.

"What?" asked Nell.

"Can't you . . . stay a little longer?" he asked awkwardly. "It's so . . . dark and lonely here."

Nell sighed. "Not as dark and lonely as it is here, believe me."

"Then stay," said Owen. "Let's just keep each other company for a while."

"I can't," said Nell. "I'm so tired, and tomorrow is my last chance . . ."

"Your last chance for what?"

"Never mind," said Nell. "I've got to go. Wish me luck, Owen. I'm going to need it."

"All right, princess," Owen said gently. "Good luck, and good night."

"Good night, Owen," Nell whispered.

The star went black, and Nell sat staring at it, feeling so lonely. How she wished she were home. She squeezed the star tightly in her hand.

"Father," she whispered, "at Castle Xandria."

She held her breath, careful not to make a sound as

the star began to glow again. Soon her father's figure came into focus. He was pacing in his study.

"I can't believe it," he was saying to someone. "What has gotten into her?"

"It's just a childish prank, sire," came Lady Fidelia's voice. "Don't take it so seriously."

"But cutting off her hair," King Einar cried, "and now this? What are we to hear next? I've half a mind to go pull her out of that school."

No! Nell cried silently. That Owen! He was going to ruin everything!

"Now, now, sire," said Lady Fidelia calmly. "No need to overreact. I'm sure a night in the dungeon will curb this little rebellious streak of hers."

The king sighed. "I hope you're right," he said. Then he rubbed his eyes tiredly. "Please leave me now, Lady Fidelia," he said. "I've work to do before I retire."

"Yes, sire," said Lady Fidelia. "Good night."

Nell heard the door close, then her father clasped his hands behind his back and strode to the window. He stood looking up at the night sky.

"Arenelle," he whispered. "How I hate to think of you in a dungeon." He raised a hand to his lips and blew a kiss to the stars. "I send my love to you, my jewel. May it keep you through the night."

A tear slipped down Nell's cheek as the speaking star went dark. She ached to throw her arms around her father, to tell him she was all right, and most of all, to tell him how she loved him.

There was a soft whir of wings, and Nell looked up. Minna appeared out of the night, her little mouth berry-stained.

Nell smiled, grateful for the little Dragon's company.

Minna dropped a cluster of berries in her lap.

"Oh, thank you," Nell said. "You're so sweet to bring them for me, but I can't eat them."

Minna looked at her worriedly.

"I know you don't understand, little friend," said Nell. "I don't either, but I have to follow the rules. We'll save them for Beauty when she wakes up."

Nell put the berries aside, her mouth watering. How she longed for just one! She was *so* hungry.

"Don't think about it," she told herself. "Keep busy."

She stood and began waving her clothes over the fire, trying to get the last bit of dampness out. Minna decided to help. Clutching Nell's underdrawers in her claws, she swooped back and forth above the flames.

Nell giggled.

"You silly little Dragon," she said affectionately.

Then, "Grawk!"

Minna swooped too low.

"Minna!" cried Nell. "Give me those!" She caught Minna in midair and pulled the flaming drawers free of her grasp. She tossed them to the ground and stomped the flames out. She picked them up and examined the scorched lace.

"Just look what you did," she snapped.

Minna looked so ashamed that Nell had to laugh.

"Never mind," she said, stepping into the singed drawers and pulling them up, "They're toasty warm at least."

Suddenly, in the distance, Nell heard a long, low howl. It sent shivers up her spine. *What is it?* she wondered. It didn't sound like a Night Thing. It didn't sound like a Banshee either. She hurried into the rest of her clothing and then sat down on her log, scanning the darkness worriedly. From opposite directions came another howl, then another and another.

"Rrronk," cried Minna, diving into her lap.

Nell sent more sticks scurrying into the fire, building it up as brightly as she could. She reached beneath her skirt and pulled out the dagger, then she glanced at Beauty. Should she try and wake her? A Dragon, even a sick one, would be a help in battling . . . whatever was out there.

There was another howl, louder and closer. Minna whimpered and Nell jumped to her feet.

"Beauty!" she cried. "Beauty!"

The Dragon didn't move a muscle.

Nell ran over and shook her.

"Beauty!" she said. "Wake up!"

Beauty's eyes flickered open, but then they rolled back in her head and closed again. She was too weak to move. Nell stroked her gently.

"All right. Just sleep and get your strength, girl," she said. "We'll be okay."

She called Minna into her arms and hunkered down

on the log again, clutching the dagger tight.

The howls came closer, and soon Nell could see dark shapes streaming across the plain. Thudding footsteps thundered, circling, just outside the ring of light. Silvery eyes reflected fire.

"Hinterbeasts," Nell whispered to Minna. "They have heads like wolves, but bodies like great cats." She looked at the tiny dagger, pulsing like a live thing in her hand. What good would it be against these great, slobbering beasts? She laid it on the ground and grabbed her pendant instead, pressing it against her heart. Then, strangely, the little dagger began to glow. A sound came from it—a silvery, tinkling melody.

The beasts stopped pacing and stared. Minna looked up at Nell curiously.

"That song!" whispered Nell. Goosebumps broke out all over her. "Father used to sing it for me when I had nightmares. He said Mother made it up for me while she was waiting for me to be born."

Nell closed her eyes and quietly, in a trembling voice, began to sing.

> "Sweet and gentle, precious child,
> Creatures great and fierce and wild
> Are but children just like you
> And their mothers love them, too.
> Open up your heart to all
> Eldearth creatures great and small
> And you'll see there's naught to fear.

So my little precious dear,
Close your eyes and drift away.
Night is but another day
Waiting to be born."

The song gave her a sense of peace and safety and she sang it over and over again. Soon Minna's breathing became soft and regular. She had fallen asleep. Behind them, Nell could hear Beauty's labored breathing, too. There was no more growling or panting. Could the beasts have gone away? She opened her eyes and then gave a startled little cry. There they were! Right in front of her!

The great beasts had crept in close around the fire. They all lay with their great chins resting on their paws, their eyes watching her, calmly, curiously.

Softly, Nell began to sing again. After a time, she got up and walked among the beasts, stroking their great heads and singing verse after verse of her mother's song to them. They watched her with great, soft eyes that slowly closed, and one by one, they drifted off to sleep.

Chapter Twenty-two

"What? What?" Nell asked drowsily. Someone was nudging her awake. Slowly she opened her eyes, then gasped to see a great pair of lavender eyes staring into hers. She sat up and blinked. Then everything came flooding back.

"Beauty!" she said. "Are you all right?"

"Grrrumm," hummed the yearling, switching her tail cheerfully.

"Thrummm," came another little voice, and Nell looked up to see Minna perched like a purple cap on Beauty's head.

"So, you two have become buddies, huh?" she said with a smile.

"Grrrumm," said Beauty again.

She looked healthier already. A pearly sheen was returning to her scales, and her eyes were bright and clear.

Nell got to her feet and looked around. "Those beasts?" she said. "Where are they?"

There was no sign of the Hinterbeasts. Had they been a dream? But no. There were big cat tracks all around the clearing and impressions in the dust where great bodies had lain. They must have gone home to . . . wherever home was.

Home.

A wave of homesickness washed over Nell. How she longed to run into her father's arms for a good morning hug. How she would love to be sitting down to one of the cook's sumptuous breakfasts! Her stomach was so empty it hurt.

Owen's words came back to her. *I'll bet you don't even know how it feels to be hungry.*

"Now I know," she said. "And I know it's a feeling no child should ever have."

"Please, miss. Have you any garbage?"

Nell whirled. A scrawny little waif of a girl stood at a distance, staring out at her from the shadows of a dusty hood. She couldn't have been much more than six or seven, and she was so thin that she seemed lost within the folds of her tattered robe.

"Who . . . who are you?" Nell cried.

"Raechel, miss," said the child, dipping her head.

"Where . . . where did you come from, Raechel?" Nell asked.

"Over there, miss," said the child.

Nell squinted. "I don't see anything," she said.

"It just be tents, miss," Raechel said. "We be Arduans." The child took a fit of coughing then, and

Nell had to wait for her to recover before the conversation could continue.

"Arduans?" Nell asked when the child had regained her breath.

"Garbage eaters, miss," said the child quietly.

"Garbage eaters!" Nell gasped. Then she was instantly ashamed of herself for she could see that her reaction had embarrassed the child.

"I'm sorry," she said. "But . . . why would you eat garbage?"

"It be all we have," said Raechel.

"But surely there must be some other way you can get food," Nell said.

"No, miss," said the child. "We don't be allowed near the villages or farms."

"Why?" asked Nell.

The child lowered her head. "Because we have the bloodpox, miss," she said in a barely audible voice.

Nell gasped. The bloodpox! Bloodpox was a dreadful disease that had ravaged Eldearth long ago, wiping out whole kingdoms.

"B-But I thought the bloodpox had been cured," she stammered. "I didn't think it existed anymore."

The child shook her head slowly.

"You be mistaken, miss," she said. She took another fit of coughing, then held out her small hand so Nell could see the raw, red sores that covered it. "See?"

Nell's heart broke to look at the little waif and to imagine Raechel's difficult life. Nell tried to remember what she knew of the bloodpox. Had it actually been cured, or had its victims simply been banished, like the Arduans, until they all died off?

"Have you any garbage, miss?" Raechel asked again.

"No," said Nell. "I'm sorry."

"All right then," said the child, but she lingered, peeking shyly out from her hood at Beauty and Minna.

"Do you like Dragons?" Nell asked.

"Yes, miss," said Raechel, shuffling her feet in the dirt, "'specially little ones."

Nell called Minna down into her arms.

"Would you like to pet her?" asked Nell.

"Oh. I don't dare, miss," said Raechel.

"Of course you do," said Nell. "Dragons can't catch the bloodpox."

"But *you* could, miss," said Raechel.

Nell hesitated, but her compassion for the child was stronger than her caution. "I'm not worried," she said.

"Are you sure, miss?" asked Raechel.

"I'm sure," said Nell.

Raechel came forward hesitantly, then reached out and scratched Minna's head.

"Thrumm," sang Minna, and the child giggled delightedly.

Nell felt a pang of guilt seeing how much joy this small pleasure gave the child. She almost wished she could give Minna to Raechel, but then, Minna wasn't hers to give, and even if she had been, Nell had grown too fond of the little Dragon to imagine ever parting with her.

Raechel glanced off into the distance and uttered a small sigh.

"Better go now," she said. "Arduans breaking camp."

"Yes," said Nell. "Your parents will be looking for you, I'm sure."

"No, miss," said Raechel quietly. "My mother not be Arduan. She never got the bloodpox. And my father be dead already."

"Oh," said Nell, swallowing hard. "I'm sorry."

"Good-bye," said the child. She started to walk away, then turned back for a last look at Minna. She giggled once again. "She be so cute," she said.

Nell had a sudden thought. "Raechel," she said. "How would you like to be able to see Minna whenever you wished?"

"How?" Raechel asked.

"This is how," said Nell. She reached beneath her skirt and pulled her speaking star out of her sack. Then she wavered, staring at it a moment. If she gave it away, she wouldn't be able to contact Owen anymore. But Owen was safe and comfortable and well fed. This little child needed some bit of joy in her life, no matter how small.

"Here," said Nell, holding the star out.

"For me, miss?" said the child.

"Yes," said Nell. "Take it."

Raechel took the star in her hand.

"What are these plains called?" Nell asked.

"This be Azwan, miss," said Raechel.

"Then look into the star and say, 'Minna, Azwan.'"

Raechel did as she was told, and soon the star began to glow.

"It's lighting up!" she cried.

"Yes," said Nell. "Keep watching."

"It be her!" Raechel said. "It be the little Dragon!"

"Yes," said Nell. "If you want to see her again, you just have to say her name and the place where she is."

"But . . . how will I know where she be?" Raechel asked.

"You should be able to find her at the Palace of Light," said Nell, "or at Castle Xandria."

Raechel stared at the star for a long time, then she looked up at Nell.

"Do it work with folk, too?" she asked.

"Why, yes," said Nell. "As long as you know where they are. If you call someone, you'll be able to see them and talk to them, and they can talk back, but they won't be able to see you."

"Even folk you haven't seen in a long time?" Raechel asked, wide-eyed.

"Yes," said Nell.

The child stared up at Nell for a moment, then she peered down into the star. Her little hands were trembling.

"Mother," she whispered softly. "Katahr Village."

The star began to glow, and after another minute a figure appeared in the center.

Raechel looked up at Nell with tears in her eyes.

"This be the best present in the whole world!" she cried. She threw her arms around Nell's waist and hugged her fiercely; then she ran off, clutching the little star to her heart.

Nell stared after her, brushing tears from her own cheeks.

"Take heart, Raechel," she whispered, more to herself than to the retreating child. "Better times are coming."

CHAPTER TWENTY-THREE

Nell washed up in the lake, then scooped a handful of water to quench the last smoldering coals of the fire. She rubbed her tired eyes and surveyed the unfamiliar countryside.

"Which way now?" she mumbled.

To her surprise, the dagger, still lying in the dirt, began to spin. Had she kicked it unknowingly, or was it helping her? It turned in three slow circles then came to a stop, pointing toward the mountains in the distance.

Nell shrugged.

"Looks like as good a direction as any," she said.

She tucked the dagger into her pouch and set off across the dusty plain, leading Beauty by her reins. She had not the heart to ask the yearling to fly again until she grew stronger. Minna fluttered overhead for a while, then hitched a ride on Beauty's head.

Nell's tongue was thick and dry, sticking to the roof of her mouth. Her stomach was so empty it was beyond hungry. It was a gnawing, aching pain in her middle. She scanned the horizon constantly, searching for some sign of the palace, but her own dizziness, and the shimmering sun, kept playing tricks on her. She saw castles, pools, trees, whole cities—only to run toward them and watch them dissolve.

As the day wore on she began to stumble and fall, and her heart grew heavy. At last she fell to the ground and just lay there, unable to rise again. Tears stung her eyes.

"I'm not going to make it," she cried. Then she remembered the dagger. Could it help again? She took it out and placed it on the ground. "Which way?" she asked.

Slowly it began to spin, three times around again, and then it stopped. Nell stared toward where it pointed, directly at the sun, hanging low now between two mountain peaks. It hurt her eyes, and she scrunched them up until they were just slits and the sun swam in her tears.

Nothing.

She brushed the tears away, then suddenly she saw something! A dark square, like a doorway, at the base of one of the mountains!

Her heart started to pound. Was it real, or just another mirage? She tucked the dagger back into her belt, struggled to her feet again, and stumbled forward.

And then it was gone!

"No, no!" Nell cried. "It has to be real!" She scrunched up her eyes again, and the doorway reappeared!

"Yes!" she cried, running forward. And then it was gone again. But this time she knew why. Each time she opened her eyes fully, the doorway disappeared, but by scrunching them, she could find it once more!

At last she reached the doorway. It was small, just big enough for her to pass through without stooping, and it kept changing colors, depending on the light. Sometimes it disappeared completely, but by moving a bit to the right or the left and squinting, she could pick it up again. Was this one of the illusions that guarded the palace? Tentatively she reached out and touched it.

It was real! It was *really* real! A shiver of excitement zipped up her spine. Nell turned to Beauty and Minna. There was no way Beauty would fit through the doorway. Nell would have to leave her behind, but Beauty was still so frail. She didn't want to leave her alone.

"Minna," she said. "Stay with Beauty. Go find food and water, and then wait for me here. I'll come back for you, I promise."

"Graw?" said Minna.

"Trust me," said Nell. "I'll be back as soon as I can. Now, here . . . take Beauty and do as I say." She held up the reins, and Minna fluttered over and grabbed them in one claw.

"That's my girl," said Nell, smiling as she watched the great white Dragon lumber off docilely behind the little purple miniature.

With a sigh of resignation Nell turned and stared at the door. She swallowed hard. What waited on the other side? She touched her pendant.

"Stay with me, Mother," she whispered; then she took a deep breath and pushed the door open.

Chapter Twenty-four

"Zow," whispered Nell, borrowing Owen's word. She found herself in a long corridor with a high, arched ceiling. It was dark, except for torches that blazed at intervals, illuminating walls that glittered like black crystal. The air was cool and everything was silent. Was she in the palace or would this corridor lead her to it?

"Is . . . Is anyone here?" Nell called.

"Anyone here . . . here . . . here . . . ," her voice echoed.

"Someone must be here," Nell mumbled to herself. "Someone must tend these torches."

Slowly she began to make her way down the corridor. There was no sound but the flutter of the torch flames and the patter of her own feet on the shining stone floor.

"H-Hello," she called out tentatively every few moments, but no one answered.

At last she heard a splashing, gurgling sound. She rounded a corner, and the passageway opened into a circular room with a sparkling fountain in its center. She swallowed with difficulty, her dry mouth thirsting for a taste.

And then a crystal goblet appeared in her hand. She looked at it in surprise.

"Hello?" she called again.

No one answered.

Am I allowed to drink? she wondered. But no. She couldn't take the chance. This was the third day. She had to reach her goal today and the Articles of Apprenticeship had clearly stated that the palace had to be gained by sunset. She couldn't be sure she had reached her goal yet. She walked over and put the goblet down on the low wall that surrounded the fountain.

Oh! The water smelled so fresh and the mist felt deliciously cool on her skin. Her mouth was so dry, her lips blistered and cracked. Maybe if she just tasted the mist . . . She leaned closer, closer . . . the fountain seemed to be drawing her in. Then, as she bent forward, the dagger in the pouch beneath her skirt dug sharply into the top of her leg. She jerked back and blinked her eyes.

"It's warning me," she whispered. "This is a test!"

She wrenched herself away from the pull of the fountain and raced across the room and into the corridor on the far side. She didn't slow until she could no longer hear the seductive splash of the water, then she stopped and leaned against the wall, her head spinning.

She patted the dagger through her skirt.

"Thanks, Owen," she whispered. He sure had been right about it being more than just a dagger.

Nell pushed on, weak and tired, but conscious that the sun outside was sinking ever lower. In time she became aware of a tantalizing aroma in the air. Food! She could smell roasting meats and baking bread. Dry as her mouth was, it flooded with saliva instantly, and her shriveled stomach began to groan.

"Please let those smells be coming from the palace," she prayed. But no. Up ahead she saw a glow of light. It was just another room in the passageway. Another temptation.

This room was like the other except that it had a great table in its center laden with every delectable food Nell could imagine.

"Don't look," she told herself. She closed her eyes and tried to walk by, but her steps led her directly to the table instead. She bumped into it and opened her eyes.

Right beneath her nose was a steaming plate of roast meat, swimming in gravy. Next to that was a basket filled with warm breads. Beyond that a huge selection of cheeses, a golden-roasted fowl surrounded by baked apples, piles of fresh fruit, cakes and pastries dripping with icing . . .

Nell groaned, her stomach begging her, egging her on. Her fingers reached out almost of their own accord and touched a soft, warm loaf of bread.

"Maybe if I just touched it to my tongue," she whispered, lifting the bread toward her mouth. "I wouldn't really be eating it if I just tasted it."

She closed her eyes, opened her mouth, and stuck out her tongue.

Aahh . . . What!? This taste wasn't warm and yeasty. It was cold and flavorless!

She opened her eyes and saw that her mother's pendant had become hooked on the bread as she lifted it to her mouth. What she had tasted was the ruby stone.

She dropped the bread and jumped back. Then she bolted from the room, clutching the stone.

"Thank you, Mother," she whispered. "Thank you."

She ran on, tripping and stumbling in her exhaustion, but worried that time was running out. She *must* be close to the palace now. There couldn't be any more temptations, could there?

Then she heard strains of music, like a lullaby, and saw another light up ahead. Her heart sank. It wasn't the palace. Just another room. Well, she would run right through this one. Nothing would make her stop!

She reached the doorway and saw that this room had a huge featherbed in its center. Bent over it, turning down the blankets, was a woman!

Nell stopped, startled to see a real person at last.

"H-Hello?" she stammered.

The woman straightened and turned, and Nell shrieked and put her hands to her mouth.

"Arenelle," said the woman, smiling warmly and putting out her arms.

"M-Mother?" gasped Nell.

"Yes," said the woman in a voice as sweet as honey. "Come in, my child. I've been waiting for you." She began to walk toward Nell, her arms still outstretched. "My baby. I've missed you so."

Nell's heart thumped wildly. Could this really be her mother? She stared at the outstretched arms, longing to run into them, but fearing a trick.

"But . . . how . . . how can you be alive?" she stammered.

"You are in a mystical place, dear," said the woman. "Anything is possible here." Then her forehead creased with concern. "Look at you. You're exhausted, you poor thing. Come rest a bit."

"I can't," said Nell. "I have to go on."

"Of course you have to go on," said the woman. "I wouldn't dream of stopping you. But there's time yet. A little rest will do you a world of good."

The woman put an arm around Nell's waist and led her over to the bed. It looked so soft and cozy, and Nell was so tired. . . .

The woman plumped up the pillows. She moved with such gentleness and grace, and she was so beautiful—exactly like the paintings of Queen Alethia. Love seemed to radiate from her very being, and Nell hungered for that love.

"There," the woman said. "Lie down now. Just for a few moments."

"I can't," said Nell. "I really have to go."

The woman looked so disappointed. "Why won't you accept my help?" she said. "I only want to care for you." She reached out and stroked Nell's cheek. Nell turned toward the warmth of the touch, craving more. The woman leaned forward and kissed her forehead. "My precious child, how I've missed you," she whispered.

"I've missed you, too," Nell whispered, "but—"

"Arenelle," said the woman. "Look at me."

Nell looked into the woman's clear blue eyes.

"Trust me, my child," the woman whispered. "I am your mother. I love you."

She pulled Nell into her arms and wrapped her in an embrace so warm and tender that Nell's heart melted.

"Mother," she whispered.

"Yes, dear," the woman murmured. "I am here."

It felt so good, so right, to be held so close, so warm, except . . .

There was a small, hard lump pressing uncomfortably against Nell's chest. Small and hard and growing colder—cold as ice.

The pendant!

Nell pulled back. This wasn't her mother! It couldn't be. If it was, the pendant would glow warm between

156

them. Instead it was cold as death—warning her.

"You're not her!" Nell cried. "You're a temptress!"

For an instant the warmth left the woman's eyes. They turned black and hard, like the glittering stones that covered the walls of the chamber. But then they changed again, and the warm smile returned.

"Don't be silly, my child," she said. "I am she. How else would I know you? Even dressed as a peasant, I knew you for my daughter."

"No," said Nell. She stepped back. "You're a temptress. You can read my heart's desire and use it against me. You know how I long for my mother. How could you pretend like that? You're the cruelest woman in the world!"

Nell turned and fled, sobbing from the room, running blindly, blindly, bouncing off the corridor walls until suddenly she burst out of the darkness and into the light.

Chapter Twenty-Five

Nell stood staring openmouthed at the most incredible building she had ever seen. It sparkled and shimmered, light bounding and rebounding off its multifaceted turrets, reflecting every color of the rainbow.

"I'm here," she whispered, shivering with awe and fear. "I've reached the Palace of Light!"

One trembling step at a time she climbed glittering crystal stairs that led to a huge pair of mirrored doors. For a moment she cowered before her own reflection. How dare she knock here, dirty little insignificant waif that she was.

But no. She *wasn't* insignificant! She had not given up and had succeeded where everyone else had failed. She had proven herself, proven that she was worthy of becoming apprentice to the Imperial Wizard.

A silver bell cord dangled before the doors. Nell reached up and tugged it, and instantly the air was filled with the ringing of a thousand crystal bells. A moment later the doors swung open and there stood a winged Sprite with silver hair and a soft blue gown. She was tall for a Sprite, almost as tall as Nell, and she had enormous blue eyes, so pale they were almost silver.

The Sprite stared at her curiously.

"Who are you?" she asked in her musical voice, "and how did you come here?"

"I am Princess Arenelle of Xandria," said Nell, dipping her head respectfully. "I have completed the quest and seek to be apprenticed to the Imperial Wizard."

The Sprite's eyes widened. "But . . . you are a girl," she said.

"Yes," said Nell. "I know."

The Sprite's lips twitched as if she were trying to hide a smile.

"You don't look like any princess I've ever seen."

"Looks can be deceiving," said Nell.

The Sprite narrowed her eyes. "This is highly irregular," she said. "The Keeper has been expecting a boy."

"All of the boys have failed the First Trial," said Nell. "I have succeeded."

This time the Sprite was unable to cover her smile.

"So I see," she said. "Well, come along then. This is certainly an interesting turn of events."

She reached a hand out to Nell, but Nell did not take it right away.

"I have two Dragons," she said, "a yearling and a demi. I left them outside of the corridor of temptations."

The Sprite nodded. "I will see to it that they are looked after," she said. "Come along now."

Nell grasped the hand, then suddenly found herself flying through a prism of light.

"Zow," she whispered.

The Sprite looked back at her with raised brows.

"An interesting expression," she said. "Rather crude for a princess, is it not?"

Nell blushed. "I'm sorry," she said. "A . . . friend taught it to me."

"A friend of low breeding it would seem," said the Sprite.

Nell bristled. "You sound like you're speaking of livestock," she said shortly. "Folk aren't *bred.*"

The Sprite smiled wryly. "Of course, my lady," she said. "Forgive me."

The corridor of light opened into a room that glittered like the interior of a jewel. The Sprite set Nell down in the center of it.

A door opened on the far side of the room and in walked the loveliest Witch Nell had ever seen. She had sparkling green eyes and pure white hair so light and silky that it floated about her like a cloud. She wore a crystal circlet on her brow and a soft, flowing gown of silver and white. She carried a wand so bright that it hurt Nell's eyes.

"My lady," said the Sprite, curtseying deeply before the Witch, "I present Princess Arenelle of Xandria."

The Witch nodded and if she was surprised by Nell's arrival, she gave no sign of it.

"Thank you, Zephyra," she said to the Sprite. "You may leave us now."

The Sprite curtseyed low again, then flew from the room.

The Witch looked at Nell. "I am Lady Aurora," she said, bowing her head, "Grand Dame Witch of the Palace of Light. I welcome you, Princess."

Nell curtseyed. "An honor to meet you," she said.

"On the contrary," said Lady Aurora, "the honor is mine. We have never before been visited by a princess. But where are my manners? You need refreshment."

Lady Aurora whisked her wand through the air. Instantly Nell's rags disappeared. She found herself dressed instead in a gown of the finest white brocade, with silver velvet slippers on her feet. She was fresh and clean from head to toe, and her shoulder-length hair was twisted up and crowned with a circlet of pearls.

"Feel better?" asked Lady Aurora.

"Much," said Nell. "Thank you."

"And now some food and drink," said the Witch.

A glass table appeared and a sleek silver chair, then a hidden door slid open in the floor and a succession of platters, pitchers, and bowls rose up from somewhere down below, each brimming with food or drink of one kind or another.

Soon a bounteous feast was piled high on the table in front of Nell. The sights and tempting aromas were almost overwhelming. Nell blinked at Lady Aurora, hardly able to believe her eyes.

"Is it . . . am I really able to eat now?" she asked. "I mean, it's not just another trick, is it?"

Lady Aurora smiled kindly. "No, dear," she said. "You have safely reached your goal. Now go ahead. Enjoy."

Nell was just about to raise a forkful of meat to her mouth when she heard a commotion.

"Come back!" someone was crying. "You're not allowed in there."

Minna zoomed into the room with Zephyra, the Sprite, close on her tail. Round and round the crystal chandelier they zoomed.

Nell stifled a giggle.

"Minna," she cried. "Come." She held out her arm, and Minna fluttered down and perched upon it, then hopped up onto Nell's shoulder.

Zephyra landed in front of Lady Aurora, huffing and puffing.

"I'm sorry, my lady," she said, bowing low. "I was trying to put her in the stable, but she got away."

Lady Aurora smiled.

"It's all right, Zephy," she said. "Nothing would surprise me today. The demi is obviously not accustomed to being separated from her mistress. She can stay."

"Is my Dragon safe?" asked Nell.

"Yes. I gave her some mash and tended her wounds. Now she's sleeping," said Zephyra. "She's a sorry-looking one, that."

"She's been sick," said Nell. "But she's getting better.

She's really a beauty if you can see past her bruises and burns."

Zephyra shrugged. "If you say so."

Lady Aurora chuckled. She waved her wand and a crystal harp appeared beside her.

"Zephy," she said. "Why don't you play for our guest? I must go to speak with the Keeper."

Zephyra sat down at the harp and began plucking the strings. The haunting music was soft and soothing. Nell put a forkful of food in her mouth, then closed her eyes and chewed blissfully.

Nell opened her eyes and bolted upright.

"What? Where am I?" she cried.

She found herself in a great silver bed, in a room that was filled with sunshine and light. Soft breezes sweet with the scent of flowers wafted in through the windows. She tossed aside her downy bed coverlet and hopped out onto a floor of cool white marble.

"Gawk?" cried Minna, who had been curled up on the other pillow of the great bed. She stretched her wings and shook the sleep from her little body.

Nell ran to the closest window and looked out. All around her were beautiful mountains, their tall peaks capped with snow. Above her the sky was clear blue, below a low cloud had settled, covering the ground like a billowy quilt. It almost looked as though the whole building was floating.

"The Palace of Light!" she whispered, remembering. Then she turned and looked back at Minna.

"But what happened?" she asked. "Last thing I recall, I was sitting at this huge table, eating. How did—"

"You fell asleep over your pudding," someone said.

Nell whirled. Stretched out on a daybed near the door, propped up on one elbow and looking rather grumpy, was Zephyra.

"Not a very ladylike sight, I'll tell you," the Sprite went on. "Are you *sure* you're a princess?"

"Yes," said Nell. "Are you sure you're a Sprite? I thought Sprites were known for their docile natures."

"I thought the same of princesses," said Zephyra.

"Well, I'm not your ordinary princess," said Nell.

"And I'm not your ordinary Sprite," said Zephyra.

Nell smiled in spite of herself. If the Imperial Wizard *did* accept her as apprentice, it was going to be interesting getting to know Zephyra.

A light rap came on the door, and then it sprang open. Lady Aurora blew in like a fresh breeze.

"Good morning," she said cheerfully. "I trust the princess slept well?"

"Oh, yes," said Nell. "I'm sorry about last night. I guess I was more tired than I knew."

Lady Aurora chuckled. "And deservedly so," she said. "No offense was taken, I assure you." She turned toward Zephyra, who had hopped out of bed and was standing at attention.

"Zephy, dear," said Lady Aurora. "Would you see to

breakfast? I'd like a word alone with the princess."

"Yes, my lady," said Zephyra, dipping her head, then soaring out of the room.

"Now, let's get you ready for the day," said Lady Aurora. She whisked her wand around, and soon Nell was washed and dressed.

"Approve?" asked Lady Aurora, pointing toward a mirrored panel on the wall.

Nell walked over and looked at herself. This gown, also white, was even lovelier than the one the night before. It was satin, with a high collar and a finely embroidered bodice. A gossamer silk cape attached to the shoulders at the back and fell to the floor, trailing out behind like a train. On her feet were white satin slippers, and a jewel-encrusted turban crowned her head.

"It's beautiful," she said.

Minna fluttered over and thrummed her admiration.

Lady Aurora smiled. "It's fun having a princess to dress," she said, then added quietly, "if only for today."

Nell looked at her.

Lady Aurora's smile faded. "I'm sorry," she said. "The Keeper refuses to see you."

Nell's mouth fell open.

"He . . . what?" she stammered.

"He says it's a waste of his time," said Lady Aurora. "He's says . . . what you ask . . . is impossible."

Chapter Twenty-six

Nell stood staring at herself in the mirror, her mind spinning, her ears burning. She turned to Lady Aurora once more.

"He can't mean it," she said. "Does he know what I've been through?"

Lady Aurora sighed. "He knows . . . how difficult the quest is," she said. "But you must understand. The Keeper is very old, very traditional, and *very* set in his ways."

"And it doesn't matter how hard I've worked to get here?" asked Nell. "*Nothing* matters except that I'm not a boy?"

Lady Aurora shook her head apologetically.

Nell began to pace, mumbling to herself and shaking her head. Then suddenly she stopped, whipped her headdress off, and tossed it to the floor.

"No!" she yelled.

"Grawk, grawk, grawk!" cried Minna.

166

Nell looked down and saw the jeweled turban hopping around the floor.

"Oh, Minna, I'm sorry," she cried, bending down to free the little Dragon from under the headdress. She picked her up, then straightened and faced Lady Aurora again.

"I can't accept this," she said. "I have to see him. You have to help me."

Lady Aurora shook her head helplessly.

"It will do no good," she said. "His mind is made up."

"Then we'll just have to unmake it," said Nell. "I didn't come all this way to be turned away without so much as an audience."

"He *won't* see you," Lady Aurora insisted.

"Then *I'll* see *him*," said Nell. "Where is he?"

Lady Aurora sucked in a deep breath and let it out slowly. "All right," she said. "Follow me. But I must warn you, he's been ill and out of sorts. I won't be responsible for what happens."

Lady Aurora led the way through a maze of beautiful corridors, crystal kaleidoscopes, which caught light and reflections, playing with them in constantly changing patterns. Nell would have been fascinated under any other circumstance. But now her heart was pounding within the walls of her chest. Her mind reeled with arguments, defenses, persuasions. She *had* to convince the Imperial Wizard to give her a chance!

At last they approached a pair of magnificent, gem-encrusted doors.

Lady Aurora turned to Nell.

"Power is channeled into the scepter through the Keeper," she said. "If he touches it, it will begin to glow brighter. Do not look directly at it. It can blind you."

Nell nodded.

"This is your last chance to change your mind," Lady Aurora warned. "I have no idea what will happen if you insist on going forward."

"I have no choice," Nell said simply.

Lady Aurora stared at her a long moment, then nodded. "All right," she said quietly. She turned and pointed her wand at the doors. Slowly they swung open, and a bright shaft of light shone out. Lady Aurora disappeared into it, and Nell followed.

"WHAT IS *THIS*?" an enraged voice bellowed.

"Grawk!" shrieked Minna. She darted from Nell's arms and flew toward the ceiling in a panic.

Nell's eyes slowly adjusted to the brilliant glow until at last she could see what was around her. The room was huge and round, like many of the others in the palace, but even more majestic. Its walls were faceted like a giant diamond. In its center, on a high platform, sat a shimmering crystal throne. On the throne sat an elderly Wizard in a long white robe. Upon his brow he wore a silver circlet with a single crystal star resting in the center of his forehead.

Beside the throne stood the scepter. Nell stared in awe at the inscription on its gleaming silver base.

GALERINN, it read in glowing script. A shiver of wonder raced up her spine. She was actually here—in the presence of Galerinn, the great Immortal who had transformed himself in order to save Eldearth.

"I TOLD YOU I WOULD NOT SEE THIS ONE!" the Wizard boomed.

Minna, who was still flapping around nervously, bumped into a wall and screeched.

The Wizard pulled out his wand and pointed at her. "Ice!" he roared.

Instantly, Minna stopped flapping and dropped to the floor with a sharp crack.

"Minna!" cried Nell. She ran over and picked the little Dragon up. She was frozen solid!

"No!" Nell cried. "What have you done to her?"

"SILENCE!" the Wizard boomed. "If she is dead, the blame is yours. You should not have come here."

Nell's knees began to shake. No breath came from Minna's rigid body. Her ice-glazed eyes looked blank and lifeless. Nell started to cry.

"Your Excellency," said Lady Aurora, "I beg your mercy. The child has come all this way. She has completed the quest. The least—"

"I SAID *SILENCE*!" the Wizard blared again.

Nell clutched Minna tightly, tears streaming down her cheeks. She was trembling with fear and sorrow and anger. She began to walk forward, one wobbly step after another.

"STAY WHERE YOU ARE!" the Wizard barked.

"No!" Nell sobbed. "I won't! Turn me to ice too if you wish, but I will not be silent."

The Wizard glowered at her a long moment, then he raised a hand and pointed at Lady Aurora.

"Leave us!" he commanded.

Lady Aurora frowned. "But, Your Excellency," she began.

"LEAVE US!" the Wizard thundered.

"Yes, Your Excellency," said Lady Aurora. She glanced worriedly at Nell, then hurried from the room. The great doors swung closed behind her.

The Wizard returned his angry gaze to Nell.

"How dare you defy me!" he said. "I am Imperial Wizard, Keeper of the Scepter, Guardian of Goodness!"

"Well," said Nell in a trembling voice, "if you ask me you're not doing a very good job."

The Wizard's eyes flew wide and his jaw dropped open.

"WHAT?" he roared.

Nell cringed, but she had come this far. She was not going to back down now.

"How can you say you are the Guardian of Goodness when you kill defenseless little creatures who have done you no harm? That's evil if you ask me. And I'll tell you something else: There's a lot more evil abroad in Eldearth."

The Wizard stared at Nell in such wild fury that she feared he might explode.

"There are folk who are hungry and sick and enslaved," Nell went on. "Even Old Mother is disappointed in you."

"Old Mother?" said the Wizard. "Who is Old Mother?"

"The oldest tree in the Oldenwood," said Nell.

"A *tree*?" said the Wizard. "You expect me to care what a tree thinks?"

"Perhaps if you did," said Nell, "you'd be doing a better job."

The Wizard looked away, his left hand clenching and unclenching the arm of his throne.

"And Lord Graieconn's forces grow stronger and crueler," Nell continued.

"Enough!" the Wizard blared. "Do you think this is news to me? Do you pretend to know more of Eldearth than I?"

Nell made no answer.

The Wizard got to his feet and paced back and forth across the throne's platform, pounding one hand into the other. At last he stopped and stared at Nell again, his expression grave.

"I am only one Wizard," he said. "I've done my best."

"Well . . . it isn't enough," Nell said boldly.

The Wizard's eyes hardened. "And what, pray tell, has all this to do with you?" he asked.

"I . . . I think I may be the Chosen One," said Nell.

The Wizard threw his head back and laughed.

"Are you mad?" he asked. "Look at you, you impudent little snip. You're nothing but a child, and a girl child at that. Do you even bear the Mark?"

"I bear . . . a Mark," said Nell.

"The Mark of the *Dove*?" the Wizard challenged.

"Well, no," said Nell. "But—"

"Then by what foolishness do you come here," he demanded, "making ridiculous accusations and claiming to be the Chosen One? Is your mind addled?"

Nell stiffened. "I was royally born and tragedy torn," she said. "I have powers beyond what is considered normal for my age and gender, and I have completed the quest successfully. Is there any other candidate who comes as close to fulfilling the prophecy?"

The Wizard did not answer. Instead he turned and stood staring in silence at the scepter.

"Let me try the scepter at least," said Nell. "Let me see if it glows in my hands. What harm can that do?"

The Wizard looked over his shoulder contemptuously. "What harm?" he said. "It can kill you, that's what harm. You can't just waltz in here and grab the scepter. You must be trained to handle it safely."

"Train me then," said Nell.

The Wizard snorted and turned his back once more.

Nell looked down at poor little Minna, cold and hard in her arms, and a shuddering sob escaped her lips. She kissed the tiny frozen head and clutched the little body to her heart. Her pendant began to glow.

It grew warmer and warmer until it was like a searing iron against her chest. Minna's body began to soften, then the little chest swelled with breath and the light returned to the demi's eyes.

"Minna!" Nell cried. "You're alive!"

"Thrummm," sang Minna.

The Wizard whirled, his eyes wide.

"How did you do that?" he demanded.

"I, um, used a counterspell," Nell fibbed.

The Wizard walked slowly down the steps of the throne's platform, staring in disbelief at Minna. He came close and looked into her eyes.

"Rrronk," said Minna, staring back at him defiantly.

The Wizard blinked. "This is highly irregular," he said. "That was a powerful spell."

"I told you," said Nell. "I have special powers."

The Wizard eyed her suspiciously.

"Yes, well . . . even so," he said, turning his back and climbing the stairs again, "you're obviously no *Chosen One*."

"How can you be so sure?" Nell demanded. "What if there is something in the prophecy we don't understand? What if I *am* the Chosen One, and you send me away? Do you want to be responsible for the prophecy going unfulfilled?"

The Wizard paused and looked back. He stared at Nell for a long moment, then he sighed heavily.

"All right," he said. "I will take you on as an apprentice."

Nell's mouth fell open.

"You . . . you will?" she stammered.

"Yes," said the Wizard, "under one condition."

"What?" asked Nell.

The Wizard smiled smugly. "That your father convey upon you the Mantle of Trust," he said.

"The what?" asked Nell.

"The Mantle of Trust," the Wizard repeated. "It is passed down from a father to the son he chooses as his heir."

"But what if a father has no son?" asked Nell.

"Then the mantle passes to the nearest male relative."

"Why not to a daughter?" asked Nell.

"Because that's the *law*," said the Wizard.

"Is it a given law or a created law?" asked Nell.

"It's *the* law," said the Wizard firmly, "and that's all that matters."

Nell sighed. "My father is as traditional as you are," she said. "He will never give me the Mantle."

The Wizard shrugged. "Well, then," he said. "It seems we are at an impasse. If you cannot convince your own father that you are worthy of the Mantle of Trust, how do you expect to convince anyone else that you are worthy of becoming Imperial Wizard?"

Nell's frown deepened. "All right," she said stubbornly. "Somehow I'll find a way." She turned toward the doors.

"And by the way," the Wizard called after her. "Your demi was never really dead."

Chapter Twenty-seven

Nell's heart leaped at the sight of the familiar landscape below. She was glad the Imperial Wizard had agreed to transport her back to the borders of Xandria magically. It seemed that the trip had only taken minutes.

"Look, Minna," she cried. "We're here!"

Minna, who was once again hitching a ride on Beauty's head, looked down and thrummed, her little tail switching merrily.

Nell stroked Beauty's neck. "Your new home is just over that next rise," she said.

Beauty winged her way upward, and then the village was in sight, nestled between the softly rolling hills, and there, on the far hill, the castle! Could it possibly have been just a few short days ago that she had left this place? It seemed months, and she felt *so* much older than the child she had been then.

"There, Beauty!" cried Nell.

Beauty soared over the village and circled once

around the castle. "Down," said Nell, tugging on the reins and guiding Beauty down right into the garden in the center of the courtyard.

Guards suddenly appeared on all the parapets, their crossbows aimed at the new arrivals.

"At ease!" Nell cried. "It is I, Princess Arenelle."

The guards lowered their bows slightly, but did not disperse.

"Send for my father if you don't believe me," Nell cried.

The captain of the guard motioned to a young knave, who went scurrying away. Moments later King Einar burst through the double doors and strode out onto the steps, the knave close on his heels. The king stared in astonishment.

"Is this some kind of an enchantment?" he bellowed.

"No, Father. It's really me," Nell cried.

"My daughter is cloistered at the Academy of Witchcraft," King Einar argued. "I just had a communication from Madame Sofia about her moments ago. You cannot be Arenelle."

Nell swallowed hard. "I'm sorry, Father, but I am not at the academy," she said. "I sent another in my place."

King Einar's brows crashed together in disbelief, and Nell glanced up at the guards uncomfortably. "Perhaps we should go inside," she said. "I have much to explain."

King Einar stomped down the stairs and over to Nell. He put a hand under her chin and tilted her head this way and that. Then he put a finger under the chain that encircled her neck and pulled the pendant free of her bodice. He stared at it, then he stared at her. He reached down and took her hand and closely examined her Charm mark. At last he signaled the guards to disperse.

"You certainly *do* have much to explain," he muttered gruffly, "starting with that haircut. Follow me."

Nell handed Beauty's strap to the knave.

"She's in need of healing," she told him. "Take her to the Dragon Master."

The knave nodded, then Nell and Minna followed King Einar into the castle. Lady Fidelia and Lord Taman came hurrying toward them across the entry hall. Lady Fidelia gasped.

"What is this?" she cried.

"It would appear that Arenelle has not been at the academy as we had been given to believe," King Einar bellowed.

Lady Fidelia flushed red.

"But . . . how—," Lord Taman began.

"I don't know how," Kind Einar interrupted, "but I am about to find out." He stormed past Lady Fidelia and Lord Taman. Lord Taman stared openmouthed at Nell. Lady Fidelia gave her a look of concern mingled with relief, then fell into step behind her.

King Einar led the way to his study, then paused at the doorway.

"I will speak with my daughter alone, Lady Fidelia," he said. "I will send for you if I need you."

Lady Fidelia nodded. "Yes, my lord," she said.

King Einar motioned Nell inside, and Minna fluttered after her. He closed the door behind them.

"Sit down," he said, pointing to one of the chairs that flanked the fireplace.

Nell took her seat silently. Minna perched on the back of her chair, and the king sat down opposite her.

"Explain," he said, crossing his arms over his chest and glaring.

"I . . . sent an imposter to the Academy of Witchcraft," Nell said quietly, "and I undertook the quest."

The king's eye's crinkled in disbelief.

"The quest," he said. "You can't mean—"

"Yes," said Nell. "I went to the Palace of Light."

The king's chin nearly hit the floor.

"What do you mean you *went to* the Palace of Light?" he demanded.

"I undertook the quest," said Nell, "and I succeeded. The Imperial Wizard is willing to take me as apprentice."

King Einar turned so red Nell thought steam would surely pour from his ears.

"This is nonsense!" he bellowed. "Who are you, coming here making these outrageous claims? I forbade my daughter to make the quest. She would never disobey me."

Nell hung her head.

"I did not want to disobey you, Father, but you left me no choice. I had a destiny to fulfill."

King Einar leaped to his feet. He came forward and leaned over Nell, placing his hand upon the pendant. Gently he pressed it to her heart.

Thump, thump. Thump, thump it went, growing warm.

Slowly the king straightened, then he staggered back and dropped into his chair. He put his head in his hands.

"It is true," he said weakly. "It is true."

When he looked up again, there were tears in his eyes.

"How could you do this, Arenelle?" he whispered. "You are my heart, my jewel. How could you wound me this way?"

Nell rose from her chair and walked over to her father. She knelt and took his hands in hers, gazing earnestly into his face.

"Please understand, Father," she said. "I love you, but I am not your jewel. A jewel is but a bauble, something to be looked at and admired, then locked away for safekeeping. I am so much more. I have a mind and a heart. I have courage and strength. I have wisdom and powers beyond my years and I want to use them to save Eldearth. You must see me for what I am, and not what you wish me to be. You must bestow upon me the Mantle of Trust and let me fulfill my destiny."

King Einar pulled back. "The Mantle of Trust?"

"Yes," said Nell. "The Imperial Wizard has set this as a condition of my apprenticeship."

"But . . . the Mantle is to be passed to my heir," said the king.

"I know," said Nell.

"But you cannot be heir to the throne," said King Einar.

Nell pulled back. "Why?" she asked.

"Because you . . . well, because—"

"Because I am a girl?"

"Well, no, of course not," King Einar blustered. "It's just that . . . I mean . . ."

"Answer me this," said Nell. "If I were a boy and the Wizard made the same request, would you hesitate to grant me the Mantle?"

The king gazed at Nell intently, then he sighed.

"I would still fear for you," he said.

"But you *would* let me go," said Nell. She took his hands again. "Father," she said, "if *you* do not have faith in me, who will?"

King Einar stared hard at Nell, then he gathered her into his arms and pressed his cheek to hers. He held her close for a long time.

"It is hard to be a good king," he whispered, "but so much harder to be a good father." At last he pulled back and gazed at her sadly, but proudly.

"A Wizard named Nell," he said with a reluctant smile. "I must admit, it does have a certain ring to it."

ABOUT THE AUTHOR

JACKIE FRENCH KOLLER is the author of more than thirty books for children and young adults, including the popular Dragonling fantasy series, available in a two-volume collector's set. Her books have garnered numerous awards and honors from the American Library Association, the International Reading Association, and many others, and have been published in several foreign languages. One of her novels was made into the movie *You Wish* for the Disney Channel. Ms. Koller, mother of three grown children, now lives on a mountain in western Massachusetts with her husband, George, and her black Lab, Cassie. She welcomes visitors to her Web site: http://www.jackiefrenchkoller.com.

9 780689 855917